The Land Beyond Summer

Brad Linaweaver's

The Land Beyond Summer

PULPLESS.com, inc.
775 East Blithedale Ave., Suite 508
Mill Valley, CA 94941, USA.
Voice & Fax: (500) 367-7353
Home Page: http://www.pulpless.com/
Business inquiries to info@pulpless.com
Editorial inquiries & submissions to
editors@pulpless.com

Pulpless.Com™ Digital Edition June 1996.
First Pulpless.Com™, Inc. Trade Edition May, 1999
Library of Congress Catalog Card Number: 98-83267
ISBN: 1-58445-003-7

Book and Cover designed by CaliPer, Inc.
Cover Illustration by John Ng © 1999 by John Ng

To Six Special Girls:
Morgan Griffin
Vanessa Koman
Amber Haslup
Kim Riley
Soleil O'Neal–Schulman
Rylla Cathryn Smith

Table of Contents

Chapter One
Crossed Fingers

Fay didn't think Anne Jeffries would be coming back after the little girl ran screaming into the woods. Having recently celebrated her thirteenth birthday, Fay felt a lot more mature than nine year old Anne; but she hadn't been patronizing about their friendship and regretted the girl's departure. There weren't many friends out here in the country, and after Anne told her story, even fewer people would care to visit the Gurney family.

"Not again," came the voice of Fay's brother, Clive. He must have discovered the problem. Older brothers couldn't help being a pest but lately he had shown a resourcefulness that was a pleasant surprise to her. Their shared problem was bringing them closer together.

The latest example of why the Gurney house was becoming a place to avoid was making noise in the old nursery. Fay joined Clive in the doorway and stared at the yellow, peeling wall paper, covered with fading pictures of white lambs and pink pigs. The pictures were moving. And the pigs were making squealing sounds.

Anne must have wandered into the nursery just in time for the unscheduled performance. She hadn't been around a week earlier for the driveway when it changed colors from white to green. And she missed the floating telephone. But the overactive wall paper had done the trick. The whole summer had been like this.

"What's going on?" Dad's voice boomed down the hall. Fay caught her brother's unhappy expression. Calming Mom and Dad after the last one had been hard enough without having to go through it again. Clive sagged under the weight of his anticipations, and seemed older than his fifteen years. But when he was worried, he seemed handsome to Fay, as though his face were meant for frowns with its square shape.

Dad appeared in the mirror hanging in the hallway that led to the nursery. Fay saw him framed in that space, with her own reflection in the lower right corner of the glass. He was still a good looking man, although slightly balding and with a middle aged paunch. She was more critical of her own appearance. She had long auburn hair, a freckled face and big glasses that she positively hated. Fay was convinced that she was the ugly duckling of the family and that she would never grow into even a fraction of her mother's natural beauty.

As Dad moved out of frame by walking down the hall, she felt guilty that she was squandering time on such idle reflections in the midst of the latest crisis. She was awfully tired of these intrusions of the bizarre into her world ... and they were coming more frequently.

Dad was breathing heavily. His face became as red as Fay's, but she was suffering from a slight sunburn. Dad hadn't been taking any sun lately. He was mad. This was not a good sign when he hadn't seen the wall paper yet. But Fay remembered that a number of bills and late notices had come in yesterday's mail. Dad had been more upset than usual about his dishonest business partners and Mom had just been upset. Clive started answering the phone to screen calls from creditors but his skill at diverting dunning calls merely provided Mom and Dad with another subject for argument. They weren't comfortable with the example they were setting for their children.

A tape recording machine took some pressure off the family. But it couldn't screen out nightmares that came alive.

And yet there was nothing in their financial difficulties that thousands, millions, of other families didn't also have to face. What made their burden so wearing was the added frustration of never knowing when the laws of nature would be thwarted, turned upside down, or just plain ignored for the sole purpose, it seemed, of giving them a hard time. Fay could take it. Clive could take it. But the way Dad stood in the doorway, trembling, his hands clenching and unclenching themselves into slowly turning fists, suggested that he might be reaching his limit.

"It's a song," he croaked. "Listen." The squealing pigs were indeed becoming rhythmic, and a low, bawing sound was added, no doubt the lamb accompaniment.

"Old MacDonald Had a Farm!" announced Clive, a little too happy with himself under the circumstances and blissfully unaware of his father's murderous expression.

Adding to the fun, Mom suddenly appeared behind her husband. It shocked Fay to see how tired she looked. She'd been dragging for weeks but her appearance had deteriorated dramatically since last night.

"Honey," she said, peering intently at the back of Dad's neck, and there was no sweetness in her voice. "It's not happening again ... is it?"

Fay wished she'd noticed the danger sign of Clive's mouth opening sooner than she did. One of his worst faults was his inability to recognize when he was on thin ice. "It's just like Fay and I told you," he told them, "we're under attack by..."

"Shut up!" said Dad in the coldest voice Clive had ever heard. He shut up. Then Dad went over to the nearest portion of crazily writhing wall paper, extracted a pocketknife and peeled off a section. The maneuver was easily accomplished because of the age and brittleness of the paper. He held the piece between two fingers, lifted it to his ear and listened. Motion eerily swam across the fragment.

Then Dad did something every bit as careless as if he'd been Clive. He passed the section of wallpaper to Mom. She held it as if it were some kind of insect that might bite her. No one said a word. 'Old MacDonald Had a Farm' continued being screamed, grunted and bleated out from the wall, and from the palm of her hand, until she sobbed and threw the paper from her. "I'm going insane!" she screamed and ran from the room. Dad was right behind her, a helpless look on his face.

"Why is Grandfather doing this to us?" asked Fay in a small voice.

"He never did things like this when he was alive," said Clive.

"Yes," agreed Fay. "He's worse than ever."

They were talking about Grandfather Donald who didn't approved of his daughter marrying someone who didn't make a lot of money. For some curious reason, Mom's father never reconciled himself to the realities of the modern world, and the requirement of two incomes for a modest family just to squeak by. His theory was that savings could be put aside from any income, no matter how meager; and that children shouldn't be used as an excuse for spending money. The irony was that he brought up his daughter to care about appearance and hygiene and health, and then criticized her expenditures in this very area as wanton luxury.

Mom talked a lot about having nothing more to do with her father, especially after Grandmother died ... but Dad never believed her sincerity. Russell and Claire Gurney were having more financial problems every year. They felt they were in no position to antagonize the wealthiest individual on either side of the family. And Grandfather was never above using his money as a stick with which to coerce the pretense of filial affection.

Mom and Dad had insisted on owning their own home. They'd seen too many of their friends who tried to rear children in apartments find more spacious accommodations in divorce court. They also believed it was good for children to grow up in the country.

Their mistake was to live in a house where Grandfather owned the mortgage. The old man had a knack for putting the best possible face on any deal. He promised them that rental prices would always be more of a problem than commuter's gasoline prices, and he assured them good terms on the grounds of "keeping the house in the family." They fell for it.

So Russell and Claire, with their newborn baby, Clive, moved in.

Adding to family togetherness was that the house was at one end of a large stretch of woods ... and Grandfather had a summer cabin at the other end. This proved to be a most unfortunate proximity. The cabin was on Pine Lake and Clive and Fay liked to go swimming there. Most of the time Grandfather was in town but they never knew when he might show up, a consummation devoutly to be avoided.

Dad's parents had been dead a long time, so Fay and Clive had known only one set of Grandparents. There was a lot to like about Grandmother Joyce, but she could only offer them so much of her time as she was preoccupied with cancer, sliding in and out of remission as a flame hisses on and off, uncertain whether or not to burn.

When she was feeling up to it, she was their idea of a perfect grandmother, spoiling them at every turn. But half the time, Grandfather would counter her kindnesses with petty nastiness he dredged up from the sour regions of the soul. It was if he kept a little bit of poison to sprinkle on every pleasure in the world.

Then one day, exactly one year before the wallpaper sang, Grandfather summoned Fay and Clive to spend the weekend with him at his cabin. Mom didn't want them to go. Dad said he was sure it would be all right, but Fay didn't tell anyone what she had heard her father say on the phone. Apparently, Grandfather Donald was willing to offer financial aid to his son-in-law, but only if the kids spent extra time with him.

As they took their favorite path through the woods, Clive became more exasperating than usual. Fay wore a red shirt. Clive had a severe attack of wit. It was bad enough going to see Grandfather Donald without listening to references about "Little Red Riding Hood"! She had to tell Clive to stop it several times before he got the message.

Grandfather was waiting for them on his wooden dock. In a way, they had been surprised to see how well he maintained it, the only dock on Pine Lake. He used it so rarely. But then everything he owned was viewed in terms of an investment. To them, he was simply providing a good diving platform.

The first time Clive had seen a picture of Charles DeGaulle in a textbook, he'd thought he was seeing a picture of Grandfather who had physical traits in common with the French general and president — both were tall and gaunt, and had the same high cheekbones and distinctive nose. Grandfather was also balding, and this increased the similarity to the picture. Clive didn't mind Mom being tall like Grandfather, or having his cheekbones, but he was grateful that there the similarity ended. Mother's features were every bit as soft as her father's were hard.

Without saying a word, Grandfather pointed at the little wooden dinghy tied to the post. Clive exchanged glances with Fay, and he could tell she was no happier than he about getting into the boat. Having come this far, it seemed the only thing to do.

Grandfather sat in the middle of the boat, facing them, and lifted the wooden oars. The only part of the boat that was metal were the two oarlocks and the wood scraped against them with a *kathunk* sound as he put the oars into the water. He rowed to the middle of the lake, leaning forward and then backward as he rowed — his posture rigidly straight — with a machine-like precision. Given his advanced years, there was hardly any change in his breathing. He'd kept himself in good shape.

Clive tried smiling at him. He looked right at his grandson but his expression remained impassive. Finally, he stopped rowing and pulled the oars in. Still there was silence, except for the *plop-plop-plop* that came from the dripping oars. The boat slowly turned in the center of the round lake, as if a needle on a compass seeking true north.

These were three very stubborn people. At times like this it was as if Fay and Clive could read each other's thoughts. Grandfather had brought them here so he would have to make the next move. Patience was rewarded. "You're not very polite," he said at last.

"Huh?" was Clive's considered response. Fay elected to withhold comment.

"You haven't even said hello to me," the old man complained.

Fay began to sputter her response, and at length calmed down sufficiently to say, "We've been waiting for you."

"I've always been a good icebreaker," said Grandfather, "if I have a titanic reason." Had he made a joke? If so, he showed no sign of recognition but instead berated his audience. "You're not to blame for the way you were reared," he said as though he were conferring a compliment.

For some time now, Clive had noticed that Grandfather was incapable of seeing the good in anything. Clive also noticed the family's increasing load of debt and felt that he should do something about it if possible. But what could he do? His few odd jobs only added up to a nice gesture. There's nothing worse than feeling equally helpless and responsible. Here on this lake, at this moment, he let himself believe that maybe, just maybe, he could bring Grandfather around to a more reasonable attitude.

"This is so beautiful here," said Clive. "You must find it very restful. Those are..." — he groped for the right word — "really nice trees." He grinned again.

"You've got to be kidding," said their elder. "When I look at those trees, I see all the money I could make if only they were mine. They fall outside my property so I can't make 'em fall! Chop 'em down, I say."

Clive let his smile fade. Fay made a little noise that sounded like *urp!* "If they were my property," she said, "I would keep them. Why own something if you don't love it?"

Grandfather ignored her and got on with the serious business of harassment: "You don't have many friends, do you children?" he asked, and there was nothing remotely friendly about the inquiry.

Not wanting to hog all the conversation, Clive waited for Fay to take the lead. She hated to be called a child. But the sight of her was all he needed to realize that she was too angry to speak. But if looks could kill....

Grandfather hadn't approved of a mutual friend of Clive and Fay's, a Japanese boy named Kenny who owned a splendid turtle collection. Grandfather visited one weekend when they were all together. Although he hadn't said anything openly racist, the tenor of his remarks left no doubt that Kenny bothered him. There was one Pearl Harbor joke too many.

"We do all right," said Clive. "We'd probably have more friends if we didn't live so far out."

Grandfather started whistling through his teeth. When he grew tired of torturing their ears, he said, "Excuses, excuses. The two of you spend too much time together for a brother and sister. Why, an unbiased observer might think you were friends. Well, I'll have to make do with the material at hand."

No one spoke for several minutes. They just sat in the boat, staring at one another. Clive's mouth was dry and he was having trouble swallowing. Fay wanted to cry but held it in. Finally, the old man got to the point: "I wanted you with me this weekend for a reason. My time on earth is drawing to a close. I see that you're confused and so I'll endeavor to explain."

"Are you sick?" asked Fay, finally breaking her silence. She didn't feel any concern but tried to make herself sound as though she did.

His answer was anything but expected: "No, I am in the prime of my strength. I am leaving this world for another, and in so doing, my body will remain behind."

Clive turned to Fay. Fay turned to Clive. Telepathy was not required for a clear reading of each other's thoughts. Grandfather had obviously flipped his lid/wasn't playing with a full deck/was one brick short of a load. All these years of being mean had finally caught up with him.

He watched them carefully the whole time and was prepared. "You think I'm crazy," he said. "I'd be concerned if you didn't. I'd worry about my contributions to the gene pool if you were so credulous as to believe what I've said without proof."

"Oh, no, Granddad," Clive began, making another attempt at diplomacy. "We believe..."

"Shut up, Clive. Observe the example of your sister and say less. The next time you speak, I remind you to address me as Grandfather. Now, you both think I'm crazy and will continue to do so for some time yet as there will be no proof of my powers until after my death. I will be leaving you a special legacy. Your parents don't deserve it. Come to think of it, neither do you ... but you're young and there's still time for training."

Clive realized the wisdom of Grandfather's having brought them to the center of the lake. If he meant to rave, they might depart more easily on land. As it was, Fay was the better swimmer although Clive could make it to shore. The problem was that their demented forebear would simply row after them.

"You shouldn't talk about Mom and Dad that way," said Fay, coldly. Clive was proud of her.

Grandfather became worse: "My daughter hasn't a brain in her head," he insisted. "If she'd been a better daughter, I'd never have let her marry a loser like your father. She fell in love with him for the same reason you once believed the stories in Sunday School."

"That's not fair," said Clive, not exactly clear what Sunday School had to do with it, but sure that when Grandfather wasn't being crazy, he was just intolerable.

"Silence!" commanded Grandfather in a terrible voice. It was as if thunder had come out of the sky. "Children are to be seen and not heard!" More proof the old man had gone off the deep end ... except that despite his protestations regarding special powers not to be revealed until after death, he could be auditioning for a magic act at this moment.

Fay was tall for her age, taking after her mother, and Clive was well proportioned and a hair taller than his sister. Despite their age and sizes, neither resisted Grandfather's command, who continued: "I'll say when next you may speak, and not a word from either of you before then!"

Clive felt something new, something cold. It was fear. Grandfather's ice-blue eyes seemed to chill the air around his head even though it was a warm summer day.

"Know this," the old man said. "I am more than a businessman. I am more than a politician. The measly amounts of money and power I have accumulated in this pathetic life enabled me to prepare for what is to come. I have studied and I am ready. It is by magic that all means of influence are checked or grow. I have the opportunity of extending my life for centuries in this paltry world, and becoming the greatest wizard of our times. Yet I reject this possibility as beneath contempt. I will have a far greater prize.

"Your parents probably think they'll inherit a tidy sum for having put up with me for all these years. Even your father has wit enough to know that I make money when the market goes down as well as when it goes up. I pay attention. I never wasted my money on frivolities, or used children as an excuse to spend and spend. Our extended family isn't all that large, you know, and I've made more than enough to guarantee everyone a good life. Ha. No one gets a dime except the two of you!"

He finally stopped talking. For a moment. Fay's body went as taut as if a string had pulled it. Clive shook his head as if he'd been slapped. Appreciating the reaction, Grandfather continued:

"The reading of the will won't concern you. It will appear that I've lost all my money except for a pitiful amount tied up in endless probate. The real fortune was converted into gold some time ago. Half is already gone. I needed to buy certain books and paraphernalia from odd corners of the world where money is never taken seriously if it comes in paper. The other half of the fortune is well hidden and will become available as you need it to perform certain tasks for me on Earth." He raised his head from them, and blinked as though coming out of a trance. "Of course, any earthly agents would do for certain requirements..." And then he noticed them again.

His claw-like hands reached out and grabbed each of them by the wrist, shaking them with surprising strength. "You are unusual for a brother and sister. Sure, you fight about little things, as all siblings do. You blame each other over stupid nonsense that no one notices except you. But when it really counts, you stick together, which is more than your parents will ever do. You are strong, both of you. I need that ...love."

After he released them, they continued holding their arms as if still in his clutches. "Now," he said, "I want you to promise that you will keep secret what I'm about to tell you. If you don't, I'll drown you in the middle of this lake and no one will ever know." He let them think about his threat before mentioning, in a more normal tone of voice, that they could speak again.

Clive had sufficient confidence in Fay's ability in water that he didn't believe for one second that Grandfather could drown her. He was more worried that if an insane person came up short of magical powers, he might make do with a gun or knife; and the jacket Grandfather was wearing was bulky enough to conceal lots of trouble. He also worried that Fay might choose this awkward moment for an inconvenient display of principle.

He need not have worried. She answered first, without hesitation. "I promise," she said while crossing her fingers inside the pocket of her jeans. Clive was so surprised at the words coming out of her mouth that she had to nudge him with her elbow to suggest it was his turn. He promised, too.

Grandfather seemed completely indifferent to whether or not the young Gurneys were being sincere. Their words were enough. Patting them on their heads, he said, "My little lambs."

Chapter Two
Goblin Dreams

That day at Pine Lake seemed to go on forever. Grandfather talked to them until the sun dropped behind the trees. Everything was bathed in red light, casting a sanguinary pall over the scene. Grandfather looked scarier than ever, as if his whole body had become a statement in blood.

Clive and Fay hung on his every word, not out of interest but from fear. Concentration did them little good, however, as Grandfather began using unfamiliar terminology. His sentences became convoluted, almost impossible to follow. Clive glanced over to see if Fay understood (despite her younger age, she had a bigger vocabulary than her brother) but it was soon apparent that she was also confused.

Granddad's sentences became even more intricate and bizarre, clearly plundered from the storehouse of some alien tongue. The words sort of crawled over the young, captive audience like bugs, and only a few had enough semblance to English for them to get inside the ears and brains.

Grandfather didn't seem to care whether he was understood or not. He was making some kind of prepared speech, addressing someone or something not immediately present. Although Clive had given up trying to make sense out of what sounded to him like gibberish, Fay was sure that it must be a foreign language. She spoke a little Spanish. From movies and TV, she had some idea of the sounds of German and French. Finally she joined her brother in surrender. This was nothing like any other language; perhaps it was a dead language, or something Grandfather was simply making up.

Suddenly it was all over. They listened to silence, broken only by their breathing, the lapping of the water and the creaking of the boat. A fish splashed off somewhere to the left, and Clive smelled something real bad.

Clive broke the spell: "Was that, like, Latin you were doing just then?" Fay glanced over with a flash of respect showing in her eyes. He'd at least tried to figure it out. Sometimes Clive surprised her.

"What would you know about Latin?" mocked the old man. "You go to an Episcopal Church!" If he bothered listening to himself he might have laughed, but Grandfather didn't listen to anybody.

"All you need to know, children," he went on, "is that I've given you something today. Something in the way of a small power that you will inherit sooner than you think ... when the house is yours."

"You're leaving us your house?" exclaimed Clive in a voice far too loud.

"In a manner of speaking, yes. But I wasn't referring to my house just then. I meant your parents' house." They stared at him. He continued: "You'll have your parents' house after they're ... divorced."

"That's a lie!" cried Fay, getting to her feet even though she knew that you're not supposed to stand up in a boat. Clive was surprised that Grandfather didn't tell her to sit down, but he just watched with those terribly cold eyes of his.

"Poor, deluded child," he said, "don't you realize how inevitable it all is? Your mother is easily hurt. Your father is easily frustrated. When you're dealing with weak people, it's only a matter of time. They would have separated a long time ago if I hadn't saved them with money. That's the only glue holding them together! I had to pay if I wanted you with me today."

This was turning into the most perfectly terrible day that Fay had ever experienced. She didn't think she could hate anyone in the whole universe more than she hated her grandparent right then. Looking at Clive, she didn't notice any change in his composure. Maybe he was hiding his emotions.

Grandfather's withered lips moved in his scarecrow head, vomiting forth more insincerity: "I sympathize with you. You want to think that the two of you are the reason they stay together. Offspring always have an inflated opinion of themselves. And when your parents break up, you'll blame yourselves. How ridiculous. Then you'll go off with your mother, and you'll see your father on weekends. Of course there will be the same tension between them after the divorce that you feel now. And guess what happens after the divorce? They'll find new people to fall in love with, and you'll hate the new people as much as you hate me!"

The scarecrow stopped talking. The sun had finished setting while he was speaking. They couldn't see the features of his face, but only the outline of his head against the darkening sky.

Leaning forward, his dark head was very close as he whispered: "Don't worry. None of what I just described will really happen to you. To the world at large, your parents will remain married; but they won't be real people. They will be objects placed in your control. They will move and walk and talk, but they won't be alive. You'll have two parental units, forged in magic and placed at your disposal, to carry out your every command. Why, it's every kid's dream!"

"No way!" said Fay. Her nightmare for years had been waking up to find that her parents had been transformed into zombies! When she'd had her first slumber party, as young as seven years old, all the little girls had tried to scare each other with ghost stories. The oldest girl had told the rest about zombies, dwelling on an old movie where a maid was forced to comb the hair of her zombie mistress over and over.

Fay could still make out her brother's face in the thickening gloom. On this lake, the dark fell as swiftly as the dropping of a curtain. Clive smiled! For the first time, Grandfather had gotten through to him with venomous offers of role reversals and blank checks. Seized by contrary impulses to laugh or scream, Fay decided to do neither. After all, the situation wasn't as bad as it seemed.

She'd discovered that her grandfather was insane, that's all. It was tragic to be sure, and perhaps she and Clive were in danger in the dark on a cold lake with this man, but none of that plumbed the abyss of dread that would open up if one word of his nonsense proved to be true. Surely Clive didn't believe it. She decided that she must be misinterpreting her brother's expression. The boy's smile was not from desire for power, but his way of dealing with the same fact that was tormenting her: Granddad was a bowl of granola.

The annoying thing about crazy people, of course, is the way they seem to know exactly what you're thinking when they are the subject of your reflections. "You don't believe me," he said again. There were no eyes to be seen in the silhouette of his head so they couldn't tell where he was looking. "By this time, one year from now, you'll know better. It's summer now. When summer comes again, then you'll see!"

Dropping the oars back into the water, he resumed rowing and kept talking, as if to himself. "There will be dreams. Then, after I die, on the coldest day we've had this whole century, the dreams will get worse. I won't haunt you — well, just enough so that you won't forget. The boy will hardly notice because that's the way of boys. But the girl will suffer. She'll feel every portion. I'll like that. And then ... and then ..." It was like a stuck record until he shouted:

"WHEN THE DREAMS COME TRUE, YOU'LL KNOW!"

"This is what he promised, isn't it?" asked Clive, staring at the awful wallpaper. "Did you dream about the nursery?"

Fay touched the wall and said, "My dreams have been a lot worse than this." She worried that even admitting that much out loud might be a kind of invitation for bigger and better nightmares.

"Maybe we should tell Mom and Dad everything," said Clive. Fay shook her head doubtfully. She had learned from bitter experience that adults had a strange way of pretending that bad things didn't really happen. The greater the unpleasantness concerning a family member, the more likely the denial. Clive and Fay had decided not to tell about the day on the lake because they weren't sure they could convince Mom of her father's mental state; and worse, they weren't at all sure how she would take it should they succeed in making her believe!

Besides, Fay's trust in her parents had been shrinking lately, especially after Dad threatened to let Kitnip die if the vet bills went any higher for a urinary tract infection, and Mom reluctantly backed him up. (Fortunately, the last treatment had been sufficient.) Clive never really believed they would let Kitnip die. He thought they were just complaining, but Fay believed. Even though he was older, there was something more trusting about Clive.

"They'll have to believe us now," he said.

"I wouldn't count on it," she said.

Their discussion was interrupted by Dad returning to the nursery. He walked straight over to Clive, grabbed him and threw him against the wall. Dad had never done anything like that before to either of them, but here he was, manhandling his son in front of his daughter. If anything, Fay was more shocked to be witnessing the violence than Clive was to be experiencing it.

Even before he started screaming that he'd had enough of Clive's practical jokes, Fay had an inkling of what was going on. Earlier, Dad had believed what he saw and heard in the nursery, just as they had. For one brief moment, Mom had believed it, too, right before she ran out of the room. The Gurney family was united in the recognition that they were victims of a curse from beyond the grave.

But legal adults, with taxes and bills to pay, cannot keep a belief in their heads for very long. They'd made themselves forget the driveway and the phone. Adults spend so much time telling each other what the world is not like, and what life can never be, that when something really strange happens they have to pretend it didn't happen. They have to blame someone or something normal for their problems, because extraordinary events make them feel like children again.

One thing Clive and Fay had learned early on, the same as all "good kids," is never to make their parents feel like children. Not if they can help it. That's what Fay was thinking as Dad started to hit Clive about the head. Suddenly there was a shriek. Fay realized the shriek had come from her.

Fay shouted something. She wasn't sure about the words but her meaning was clear enough. She was begging Dad to stop. But it was like screaming into a vacuum.

She watched what was going on with a queer feeling of disinterest. It was like watching television. She could imagine what had happened: Mom had convinced Dad that what both of them knew to be true couldn't have happened, and therefore it must be one of Clive's "stupid practical jokes."

Fay had warned Clive for years to cut out such stuff. He'd finally stopped, but the damage was already done. Now Dad was taking out all his bottled up frustration on his son. Then Mom could blame Dad for it afterwards, even though she might have pushed him in the direction of blaming his son. And it would be one more reason for the divorce, helping to make the prophecy come true.

These dark thoughts multiplied as quickly as cancer cells until Fay had a tumor of anger in her chest to match the scene she was watching. She felt her emotions with an explosion of violence, coming over her like a tidal wave, filling her lungs so that she couldn't breathe. She had to do something! Without thinking, she ran forward, an ungainly whirl of arms and legs, trying to pull Dad away. He didn't turn his anger on her. He was focused on Clive. She could have been a vagrant breeze or a mosquito for all the good she did.

As if one unbroken motion, she kept moving. But now she was outside, and still running, headed for the woods. The dog and cat were playing in the side yard as she ran past. Since the pets had grown up together, as puppy and kitten, it wasn't surprising that they got along as well as they did. Fay wondered, in passing, why people couldn't be as reasonable as animals.

Wolf — the name Clive gave the medium-sized German shepherd — looked up from Kitnip (christened by Fay). The cat's paws were resting on the dog's nose, claws tactfully withdrawn. Playfully, she grabbed at Wolf's silver-grey head with her black paws as the dog pulled away to see what was happening with Fay. Wolf followed Fay into the woods. Kitnip rolled over, stretched, and found something better to do.

Fay didn't notice the dog close behind her. She was making a lot of noise as she crashed through bushes, oblivious to the danger of low hanging branches. She was wearing shorts and cut herself several times, on both arms and legs, but was too upset to notice.

She hadn't gone very far before she tripped over a large, gnarled root, and hurt herself in the fall. Turning to rub her injured ankle, she noticed Wolf for the first time. She was glad he was there. Rubbing him on his shaggy neck helped calm her down — and helped her to ignore the pain. After a minute of this, she resumed normal breathing. Rolling over on her side, she convinced the dog that all was well and it was time to play again.

"You're a good boy," she said to the eager red tongue licking her face. "I haven't broken my glasses so I don't need you knocking them off." Rubbing the dog behind the ears and then under his neck made her feel better.

She was very tired, feeling as if she hadn't had a good night's sleep since the summer began. Normally the extra activity of running and especially swimming would be more than adequate to provide her with uncounted hours of untroubled rest. But this summer had marked the onslaught of bad dreams. Sometimes they would relent, and she'd start to relax again, but they would lie in wait for her and when her guard was down they'd return, more vivid and disturbing than ever.

Exhaustion stole over her and she let herself think that perhaps the woods might be a safe place to take a nap, away from the family, away from Clive's suffering and the crazy wallpaper and everything else. In a moment, she was asleep.

A new dream was waiting for her. She had felt herself walking along a path in the previous ones. She would stop or get off the path when she saw something interesting. This time she seemed to be drifting through the air. She could see her body down below, where she was sleeping on the ground. Except that the trees around her seemed strangely shaped, and were very odd colors for trees — black and purple.

A yellow fog rose up from the ground, as quickly as a thought, and covered everything. She became aware of box-like shapes suspended in space between her and the fog. These objects turned slightly, as if in a breeze, except there was no breeze.

As she floated closer, she could make out that the boxes were not solid cubes as she had first assumed. They were cages. Two of them were nearly touching, and as they continued to turn she was able to see the prisoners: Mom and Dad!

There was something different about them. She noticed a quality that reminded her of the time when they still cared about each other. Fay wanted to weep, but she wasn't sure this second body of hers, this dream body, could cry. Nor could she speak or call out to them.

But there was one sensation she could feel. It suddenly became cold — colder than all the snow and ice of the Arctic and Antarctic combined. The edges of her dream shivered and the yellow fog turned into ice crystals. The cages were covered with frost, turning from blue to white. Then they exploded into a million pieces!

Mom and Dad fell through the silent sky in slow motion. She followed them down until they started drifting apart. Then she stayed with her father until he landed in a field of wheat where he picked up a scythe and started swinging it with long, sure strokes.

A voice without humanity blasted her senses, threatening to shatter the frozen remnants of her consciousness:

"Your father reaps wheat for a city. He sweats in noon sun. He has been at the task for a long while and cannot remember ever stopping, or needing to stop. He does not remember his name. He only knows that he must go on....

His legs and arms have learned the way, so he doesn't think about the work. He must swing the blade and cut the wheat for the good of his family and for himself. He has faith that if he does a good job, he will be allowed to rest — soon leaden legs can stop moving; soon tired eyes can close; soon he can apply himself to the serious task of sleeping without dreams.

Inside the city, Grandfather watches. He mutters to himself that the worker in the field is not nearly industrious enough and there will be punishment if he doesn't shape up.

The wheat is golden in the sun. Your father thinks this a pretty color. The golden glow fills his eyes with beauty. He collapses and dies. Grandfather decides that your father has found his destiny ... as fertilizer. But one day, the unexpected occurs. Sprouting from the exact spot where the reaper stood, there grows a gigantic weed.

Your mother appears, surrounded by little hopping men who tear at her disheveled clothes. She is battered and bruised. She cries out to the weed that it's a little late to put it all back together again. Then she begins cursing the city. Grandfather informs her that soon she will join her husband and the two of them will make a lovely couple."

The picture went black. Fay wanted to scream but something prevented her. The dead voice was gone, replaced by the recognizable tones of Grandfather saying: "If they can stop loving each other, they can stop loving you."

Chapter Three
New Parents On The Block

She woke up to a warm summer breeze caressing her face, and Wolf curled up next to her, head on the young girl's stomach. Directly overhead was a white cloud, as bright as a piece of cotton under a lamp. She thought of the trees as high, green reefs way down below the vast, blue ocean that was the sky. With sunlight glinting off her glasses, she felt like a silver scaled fish, hidden at the bottom where it was safe.

For one wonderful moment, she forgot who she was. Then memory came back, as cruel as ever.

Was this what it meant to come of age? To collect all your bad days and make a garment out of them, a hair shirt that you'd never neglect to wear — always chafing under the specially woven cloth of hatred that made warm days feel bitterly cold and cool days feel unbearably hot? To never have a moment of joy but that it was spoiled by memories of ill treatment and mean spirits. And most important of all: never to forgive.

"I wish I could be like you," she said to Wolf, patting him on the head. But even as the words came out she realized that she didn't really mean it. Human happiness was tied to human unhappiness. Desiring a state of animal consciousness was just another form of suicide. Fay was mature enough to realize that her happiness had been sabotaged by family bickering, but that it was up to her to deal with it.

She tried to think back to a time when the family had been happy as a family. If she could find the exact moment when everything started to go bad, then she could formulate a plan for correcting their mistakes. Only that was easier said than done. When life was going well, one didn't notice the bits and pieces that went to make up a good day.

Idly picking up a broken branch and swinging it, Fay mused over the age-old problem of the deficiencies of joy. Wolf regarded her hand hopefully, expecting at any moment that she would throw the stick. But she kept swinging it.

"Let me see," she said aloud. One of the many pleasures in having a pet was that you could talk to yourself but pretend you had an audience. "We'll make a list. There must be at least one good time we had together, when we were all happy."

Wolf barked, and she looked up from the ground to notice him wagging his tail. It's as if he were saying that she was passing up an opportunity to have a good time right here and now. "Oh, all right," she said, as if he'd actually spoken. "Go fetch it, boy!" And she threw the stick. It didn't go very far before bouncing off a tree.

"I'll throw," she said as he brought her the stick, "but you'll have to help me remember." She threw again. "The picnics we used to have," she cried gaily. "Those were happy. We all liked those." The stick was in her hand again. She decided this was a better game than watching Dad beat up Clive.

"Let's pick another time," she continued, throwing the stick again. "Swimming! Dad taught me." She remembered his strong arms around her in the water, holding her up, and there was something else about the two of them that day, alone in the pool with the sun baking their backs ... something that quivered just beyond the rim of consciousness.

She'd been afraid of the water before he taught her to swim. They'd spent the whole summer with him helping her first to relax, then to lose her fear as she slid into the water's smooth embrace.

Clive learned to swim at a much younger age than his sister, except that he could never really float on his back except by doing a little kick to keep himself moving. Fay would always cherish the day Dad and she could show off that she'd learned to float on her back while completely still, like a cork floating in a bottle.

"He doesn't dive as good as I do," she said to Wolf, as the dog returned with stick in mouth and wagging tail. "I mean as well as I do. You do insist on grammar, don't you, boy? And my diving's the best! Poor Clive usually does a bellyflop when...." She stopped short. All she could think was poor Clive.

"Well, at least we're not homeless," she muttered, retrieving the stick and throwing it again. This time when Wolf returned she brushed the stick aside. This wasn't going at all well. Here she was, hiding in the woods from her family; even hiding from her brother when he needed her the most. She didn't think of herself as a coward, but try as she might there was no good light she could throw on her behavior.

"Come on boy," she said, half under her breath, starting back. As the girl and dog headed for home, her mind was racing a mile a minute.

She remembered how close Dad and Clive had always been, so much closer than she was to Dad...or to Mom, for that matter. There was something in her that shied away from too much love. There was something unstable about any emotion that burned too brightly. One minute it could warm you but the next you'd have third degree burns from a hate that would never die.

The pictures flashing through her mind were perfect snap-shots of Dad and Clive, Clive and Dad...playing baseball, fishing, going to the movies when the feature was something she didn't want to see, smiling, laughing. But then she caught herself in the act of editing reality with an overly positive slant.

Mom and Dad tried to put a good face on things when their fortunes took a nosedive. They tried to do more family activities that didn't cost a lot of money, and Fay did her best to get into the spirit of fun they were so desperately trying to manufacture.

Now it came to this: Dad finally taking his rage out on Clive! Not because of a few practical jokes but because Clive had never masked his unhappiness at the turn in fortunes. The family had been fortunate about basic necessities. But luxuries were put in second place. Dinnertime became blander and healthier. Clothes were bought secondhand or from the discount stores. They dropped cable and went back to what Mom called "regular TV." Fay assumed they were fortunate to have TV at all. In contrast, Clive seemed to feel the good times were his due.

Wrestling over the problem, she wouldn't have been any more surprised if Dad had turned into a werewolf than to see him beat Clive for no reason. Money was not the god to Dad or Mom that it had been to Grandfather. Poverty was insufficient to explain the violence.

Grandfather. That was the issue, not money but Grandfather! They were living under his shadow. The supernatural manifestations proved the old man's crazy ideas had been true, at least in some respects. Fay and Clive could accept the intrusion of another world, another order of being, in a manner that their parents never could. For Mom and Dad, it was the last straw; one final proof of their loss of control.

Wanting desperately to forgive her parents, Fay realized that even magical curses from other worlds didn't excuse the mistakes of adults. Things had gone to hell long before Grandfather died. Magic couldn't take the blame ultimately, she reasoned. If there were such a thing as bad supernatural forces, there must be good ones as well. She was sure of this on the grounds that not everything she was taught in Sunday School could be false.

She was mulling over these questions as she emerged from the woods. Then she noticed a pile of wadded up paper over by the barbecue grill. As she drew near, she recognized the final resting place of the troublesome wallpaper.

As she cautiously approached her house, she heard singing. The music didn't come from the paper at her feet, fortunately. It came from the kitchen and it was the most pleasant sound she'd heard all day. Mom was singing! She had a very good voice. It had been such a long time since she last sang that Fay had forgotten how much she enjoyed it.

The next surprise was waiting for her in the side yard. Dad was watering the grass, in itself unremarkable (although he had trusted Clive with the chore for some while) except that he was whistling while he did it. Mom and Dad were doing a duet! And they were in tune....

Fay started in the direction of her parents, as if in some kind of trance, when she felt a hand on her arm. Turning around, she saw Clive. He had a black eye and his lower lip was swollen, caked in blood.

"What happened?" she asked, knowing the question seemed foolish when she could see his appearance.

"You won't believe it," he whispered, indicating right away that he was on the same wavelength with her. He pulled her toward the red brick well that stood off by itself while affording an excellent view of the front of the house. Wolf followed along until he saw Kitnip running after something small and furry, and joined the chase.

The Gurneys were proud of their well water. They were far enough off the beaten track out here that it would be a major inconvenience to pipe in county water. Besides, the old fashioned design had been perfect for Clive when he was growing up and pretending the well was a fort. Lying at the bottom of the dark water were the remains of toy soldiers sacrificed to a young boy's most furiously imagined battles. Now he used the "fort" as a location to plan strategy in a real battle.

As they crouched down behind the red bricks, he allowed himself to speak above a whisper, but his voice was still low and he was so near that she could smell Trident cinnamon gum on his breath. "They mustn't hear us," he said.

"Your face..." Fay began. "Dad did that."

"Well, it wasn't Mom, but she didn't do anything to stop him."

"Maybe she didn't hear..."

"She heard, all right. But that's not our problem anymore.

Grandfather did what he said."

"Huh?"

"After you ran away, Dad really started hurting me. He called me names, a lot of sick stuff. Right after he punched me he called me a mental cripple and a moron."

"No, no," was all that Fay could get out.

"Yeah, I'm just glad they didn't say anything about you." This last was a true revelation for Fay. In the last few hours she'd been brought closer than ever to her brother.

"You defended me after I ran away?" she asked.

He scrutinized her before insisting, in a voice as firm as Dad used to have, "You did the right thing. Who knows what might have happened if you'd stayed? Dad started beating on the walls of the nursery, trying to pull the wallpaper off with his fingernails. He cut a finger on the head of an old nail still in the wall. When he realized he was bleeding, he seemed to calm down a little. Then he got some tools and started scraping the paper off and running outside with it. He said he was going to burn it but he never did."

"Why not?"

"Because all of a sudden, weird sounds started coming from a brand new place." Fay's eyes were wide. He seemed almost embarrassed to continue, but he did: "The hall bathroom sort of exploded. Dad went to investigate. He came back giggling...."

"What?"

"Yeah, so I went to look and heard a gurgling voice. Fay, it was the toilet reciting the Gettysburg Address."

"Oh, I don't believe you!" Fay had heard enough. She stood up.

"No, I'm sure that's what it was. I had to memorize it in Civics."

"The toilet?" She would have left right then but he grabbed her arm and pulled her down so hard she fell on her bad ankle. Clive was considerably stronger.

She cried out in pain but he didn't seem to notice. He kept

telling his story: "Dad said he was going to burn the whole house down. I've never been so scared. Mom came out of the bedroom then, screaming at him. They started wrestling, I mean he pushed her, not hard like he was doing with me, but a push, and she let him have it, I couldn't believe it. She really hit him hard, and they fell."

Taking a moment to catch his breath, Clive seemed so miserable that it seemed indecent to doubt his word. Fay was staring at him again. She'd forgotten her pain and at least had changed her position so that she wasn't sitting on her foot.

Clive continued: "Mom finally broke away from him and got up. She said today was it. She wouldn't take any more and she was getting a divorce. She said we live in a No Fault state and she could get the divorce whether he liked it or not, and said their names are together on everything. He laughed at her. He told her it was fine with him but she wouldn't get anything because he was going to burn everything!"

"Jeezus," said Fay. There were tears in her eyes.

"Yeah, and then...." He made a face as he swallowed his gum. "They disappeared." He waited for her to respond in some way but Fay just continued to stare. He tried again: "Right in front of me. They vanished."

Fay came out of her trance and asked the obvious question: "Then who are *they*?" She pointed at the house. She wanted to do something with her hands.

He didn't need to answer. He only had to wait long enough for her to remember the day they spent with Grandfather on Pine Lake when the old man made them a promise. Mom and Dad did the rest.

Clive got into a crouching position so that he could peer over the rim of the well. Fay rubbed her ankle before deciding to do the same. Both of them watched the figure that looked like Dad watering the grass. They saw the figure that looked like Mom singing at the kitchen window.

"Who are they?" Fay asked again.

"I don't know. But suddenly the TV set came on and we had the Nickelodeon channel again. Or was it TV Land?"

"But we lost cable!"

"I know, I know, but we got it back. Grandfather's powers are awesome. The TV started playing *The Donna Reed Show*. I couldn't think of anything to do. I stood there like an idiot, watching the TV, and then the two of them appeared."

"You mean Mom and Dad reappeared."

"No! I mean two different people appeared; they just happen to look like Mom and Dad. This is exactly what Granddad said would happen."

Clive and Fay continued staring at the kitchen window for a long time. The situation struck Fay as equally horrible and absurd. After what he had experienced, Clive was too numb to feel anything.

"It's creepy," said Clive, "but while Dad was hitting me, I felt maybe I could forgive him one day. The minute he stopped and I got away from him, it was completely different. Like, the worst hatred I've ever felt. I wanted him dead. And the way Mom didn't do anything, when she had to hear, I wanted her dead, too. I would have wished them both away if I could."

"And then they were gone," Fay finished for him. On top of everything else, she had a headache. The nearest aspirin was waiting in unexplored territory. For the first time, she put her arm around Clive, the only real family she had now. He didn't seem to notice. "I wonder what's next?" asked Fay.

They held each other tight and tried very hard to think of something to do.

Chapter Four
A Letter From Mrs. Norse

"Maybe we're lucky," said Clive after reflection, "that the TV wasn't playing *The Simpsons*."

"Or *South Park*," said Fay, getting into the spirit.

"Or *The Addams Family*."

"TV or movie?" Fay caught herself. "This is completely unreal."

"Remember what Grandfather said would happen," Clive reminded her.

Fay's eyes opened wider. "They'd take orders from us?"

"Yeah." They gave each other that special look they had when they were going to do some mischief. Fay momentarily forgot her dread, and Clive took the initiative.

She followed him as they began a slow, deliberate march toward Dad. "Hi kids!" he called out cheerily, continuing to water the plants.

"Hello, father," Clive answered somewhat stiffly. "Looks to me like the grass over there could use some water." He pointed at a brown patch of dirt.

"OK," said Dad, turning in their direction while continuing to hold the hose. The water splashed both of them before they could jump out of the way.

Fay laughed. Clive frowned and said a bad word. "Well," said Fay, still giggling a little. "Now it's my turn."

"Dad," she said. "His head didn't turn. "Dad!" she said in a louder voice. Still nothing. "I want you to turn off the water." Absolutely nothing.

"He doesn't hear you," answered Clive. "Let me try again." He walked up close to the man who bore the aspect of his father and said, in as parental a tone of voice as he could muster, "You've done enough watering for today." Dad dropped the hose, walked over to the side of the house, turned off the faucet, then went into the utility room. Clive and Fay looked at each other.

"I think I understand," said Fay. "You can control Dad, which means...."

"You can control Mom!" Clive finished. "Granddad never said exactly how we would handle them. Maybe we're each allowed one. It makes sense for you to have Mom."

While her brother was talking, the unfortunate choice of wording penetrated deep into Fay, like a needle vaccinating her with cruelty. These people, whatever they were, only appeared to be Mom and Dad. Surely Clive hadn't forgotten that. Why, he had seen their parents whisked away in front of their nose.

Glancing over at her brother, she saw his eyes shining and a peculiar smile, like the expression he'd had on the lake. Some old quotation slouched toward her conscious mind, waiting to be born: was it the wheel turns or the worm turns? She wasn't sure.

Clive continued exploring the myriad possibilities: "What if we tell them to do opposite things? You know, one's supposed to turn on a light and the other turns it off."

"We don't know yet if the ... person who looks like Mom will obey me, Clive."

"Oh, she's gotta. Nothing else makes sense. Hey, you won't be able to tell on me anymore!" His smile was becoming actively unpleasant. "No more: Clive took my radio and it's his turn to walk the dog." He adopted a shrill sing-song voice that was unlike her own in any way, but seemed to be his generic choice for the portrayal of sisters.

"You won't be able to tell on me either," she answered slowly and with great dignity.

A wise man knows when to change the subject. "Let's go in the house," he suggested, "and find out what we can get away with."

She wasn't about to deny that her curiosity was fully the match of her sibling's. But she preferred that he pester her to do the dirty deed. There was something comforting in the redistribution of guilt and pain. If she'd been an only child, she was sure she would still test "Mom"; but now, more than ever, she was grateful to have a brother.

Clive, for his part, was glad of Fay's presence. This was no time to be alone. His bravado was tied to her reactions in a dozen ways he couldn't properly articulate. If she was all the family he'd have from this moment on, then he realized he could have done a lot worse. He saw value in her he'd somehow missed before.

As they sensed themselves slipping into an ever more uncertain universe, neither wanted to admit to fear. With a tentativeness worthy of a young suitor, Clive held out his hand to Fay. Coming from him, the gesture was so unexpected that at first she didn't recognize the nature of it. He wasn't grabbing or pushing; he was offering. She took his hand.

They walked to the house. One sign of normality waited for them, panting: Wolf. Fay preferred Kitnip but she liked Wolf. She often joked that she was bi-petual.

She had no doubt that Wolf was real. Besides, she figured that Clive's bond to the animal was so strong that he'd pick up on anything wrong. Yet he happily embraced the dog without a second thought. Fay looked around for Kitnip but the cat was nowhere to be found. Perhaps feline instincts sounded a warning when the cosmic axis tilted.

Mom and Dad came out of the kitchen together, arm in arm, smiling identical smiles. "How's my little darlings?" asked Dad.

"Ready for lunch yet?" asked Mom.

"Try it," whispered Clive insistently.

"Give me a minute," hissed Fay. She felt more uncomfortable than the time she'd celebrated her eleventh birthday with her first period.

The doppelgängers had some traits in common with real parents: "Keeping secrets from your old man?" asked the man who looked like Dad.

"Isn't it delightful, dear?" said the woman who looked like Mom. "They're playing some kind of game."

Sometimes Clive was given books by their Aunt Miner who assumed that because of his age and good grades that he liked to read. Inevitably, these gifts found their way into Fay's hands.

When reading some of the stories in the works of Edgar Allan Poe, she had been fascinated by the title, "The Imp of the Perverse." She didn't fully understand the story but she grasped the central idea well enough: to do something wrong for wrong's sake. That's how she felt about being made mistress over her own parents. But her feelings were for real parents, not imposters who seemed to be taking their cues from 1950's TV reruns.

Impatient over sisterly scruples, Clive decided to force the issue. "Hey, Dad, give Mom a big wet kiss. And pull up her dress, too." Dad crossed the short distance and had his hands on her.

Without thinking about it, Fay gave a counter-order: "No, don't let him." Mom started pushing him away.

"Just like they were really here," said Clive, impressed by the demonstration.

Fay gave her brother a dirty look. Now that she had started, there was no reason to stop: "Uh, Mom, you know how it's my turn today to get the mail?"

"Now, now, you're not going to dump your chores on your brother?" asked Dad, beaming.

"She's talking to Mom," said Clive in a very cold voice. "You keep out of it."

Fay would have been shocked except that Dad smiled and stopped talking. There was not the shadow of a hint of anything sinister in that smile. It was just so pleasant that it made Fay's headache worse to look at it. Dad lifted a pipe to his mouth. This was most remarkable, too, as Russell Gurney had stopped smoking before Fay was born.

"That's correct, dear," said Mom, completely unfazed by husband or son. "And if old Mr. Clock is on time today, the mailman should be arriving any moment."

"OK, Mom," Fay pursued the objective, "I want you to get the mail in my place. But first, I'd like one of your aspirins for my headache. And not a half one like you usually give me. My stomach isn't bothered by a whole aspirin."

There was something gratifying about the alacrity with which Mom fulfilled her assignment. Nor was she a robot without initiative; she provided Fay a glass of water without being asked. Then she opened the screen door and walked out to the mailbox where she stood silently, a reliable sentry, awaiting the representative of Federal authority.

"Wow!" said Clive.

"Shall I serve lunch?" asked Dad. He couldn't have been friendlier. "But first shall I turn on the television?"

Neither request struck Clive as unwelcome and he assumed these questions were addressed to the son. He nodded. Dad went over to the TV set and turned on a channel showing old episodes of *Superman*. As Dad flipped through channels with the remote control, Clive observed: "We even have premium cable, now. This is as cool as having a satellite dish." Finally Dad stopped on a channel that seemed to be featuring a special on static and snow. He walked into the kitchen and began puttering around with lunch.

"Great show," said Fay. The hissssssss grew louder. Clive was on his way to change the channel when a picture came into focus. It looked like the Public Broadcasting System with Mr. Wizard ... except there was someone else performing one of the do-it-yourself experiments.

Fay took Clive aside, pleased to note that he was more pliable than he'd ever been, responding easily to her touch. "How much longer is this going on?" she asked. "They're not Mom and Dad."

Clive nodded. "They're better."

"Clive!" She didn't like the emotions bubbling up in her chest.

She didn't want to agree. She wanted to love her parents. But it was better to feel anger than fear.

He realized that he'd gone too far. "We've got to make the best of the situation, don't we?" he asked.

"There's no escape from Grandfather," she answered.

Clive was crestfallen. It was as if he had actually made himself forget, however briefly, the incredible reality that was Grandfather Donald. If the man could do all this after he was dead, what else did he have in store for them?

Fay remembered the odd words he had spoken in the boat. The style in which he had spoken the spell or chant, or whatever it was, disturbed her more than the idea he was using magic. In fact, now that she was reminiscing, she realized that she'd always been put off by Grandfather's mannerisms. Even the arch of an eyebrow when he was trying to be mysterious could be annoying.

As she watched Clive reveling in his newfound power, she caught some of Grandfather's expressions on her brother's face. Or was she only imagining them? But they were all family, after all — and there must be times when she couldn't bear to study her own reflection.

People couldn't help having characteristic gestures and expressions and ways of speaking. Fay knew it was ridiculous to dislike someone on that basis. As she studied Clive's face, her distaste for familiarity was replaced by comfort in those same qualities. She'd never thought about these things before, but what told her right away that "Mom" and "Dad" were not Mom and Dad was the complete absence of their distinctive selves.

The replacements weren't robots. They were caricatures of someone else, with fake personalities. Leave it to Grandfather to poison any gift, even one that was already coming with strings attached.

"I hear him!" said Clive.

"Who?" asked Fay, but then she stopped short. She heard him, too. That wasn't Mr. Wizard speaking on the television. That was Grandfather. "Today's experiment," he said, holding up a beaker filled with dry ice, white steam rising as it slowly melted at room temperature, "is to settle once and for all, Mr. and Mrs. America, whether your kids have rights. Especially when the economy sucks! Or is it the best economy of all time? Who knows? Who cares? When your darlings are real little, you don't pretend they have any rights, any more than I'd say this dry ice has rights."

He lit a burner and, with a remarkably ugly Betty Crocker potholder, held the beaker over the flame. The dry ice steamed away to nothing, leaving a halo of white mist around Grandfather's head.

"If something's your property," he instructed the home audience, "you can do what you want with it. If your offspring's your property, you see the interesting possibilities. On the other hand, if you say kids got rights, think what that means! Can they enter into contracts? Will they keep their word any better than you do? Can they consent to what they actually want at any given moment of a given day, hmmmmm?"

Walking over to the TV set, Clive turned it off and gave Dad the bad news: "Sorry, guy, I've changed my mind. You can't watch TV after all."

"Whatever you say, son," came his cheery voice. But there was a louder banging of pots and pans.

As if on cue, the mail truck arrived. Fay watched Mom take the letters, smile and wave goodbye to Ed, their regular mailman. He wouldn't notice anything different if Mom had been standing in the nude with antlers on her head.

"Mail's here," Mom chirped unnecessarily as the screen door banged shut behind her.

"What is it?" asked Dad, coming out of the kitchen, wearing an apron.

"Why look, it's bills!" said Mom. She couldn't have been happier if she'd just won the Publisher Clearinghouse millions.

"And junk mail, too!" said Dad. He sounded so happy that Clive expected him to burst out laughing at any moment. Before the situation deteriorated any further, there was a surprise in the mail.

"There's a letter for our little ones," Mom beamed.

"What? For both of us?" asked Clive. After years of strenuous effort, most of the relatives had been trained to treat brother and sister as individuals, even in such trifling matters as addressing correspondence. (Aunt Miner remained the exception.) Fay grabbed the letter and showed the envelope to Clive. The return address read:

MRS. NORSE
HOUSE OF THE CAT
AUTUMN, TENTH CYCLE

There was no zip code. As for the rest of the letter, it appeared completely normal. There was a real stamp, with its ridiculously high price. The postmark showed that, whatever the return address said, the letter had been mailed within the state.

"So open it already," said Clive.

She whispered in his ear, but so softly that he couldn't make out the words. He was about to ask her to repeat herself when Mom entered the fray with: "Why don't you join me in the kitchen, Pappa bear, so that our baby bears can read their letter in peace?"

"Sure thing, honey-lamb," he said, "but it's only fair to warn you, I'm making soup to go with your sandwiches."

"Did you make it yourself?" she asked, headed for the door.

"Opened two cans, which means it's home-blended," he replied, following her, and saying one thing more — something that sounded suspiciously like, "Mmmmmmmmmmm mmmmmmmmm good."

"I don't think I can stand much more," said Clive.

"Me neither," agreed his sister. "Let's see what's in the letter." She tore it open. Something black poured out.

The room disappeared.

Chapter Five
Unsympathetic Magic

The door to the porch was standing open, and Wolf entered the house just in time to see Clive and Fay vanish. Just as quickly Wolf turned tail and was out the door in a flash of fur and doggie toenails making a tic-tac staccato on the asphalt driveway. Kitnip had chosen this moment to reappear and the two animals collided in a most unbecoming way.

Naturally the cat recovered her dignity first, but before she could withdraw, a long white hand thrust out and grabbed her by the tail. It was Mom. Except that neither animal had been confused by the interlopers who simply didn't smell right. But Fay and Clive had still been around and there was food, so why leave? Pets are notoriously practical about such matters.

While the Mom person was busy subduing Wolf with her other hand, an opportunity presented itself for Kitnip to use her claws. She made a nice, long scratch deep in the flesh of the upper arm. Ungratifyingly, there was not a drop of blood; nor did the woman show any pain. Instead, she got mad and Kitnip might have wondered if this had been a wise expenditure of one of her lives. Mom let go of Wolf, who wasted no time making a run for it. Meanwhile, she swung Kitnip through the air.

Dizzy though she was, Kitnip managed to bite Mom, but fangs were no more effective than claws had been. Mom got the cat by the scruff of the neck and that was that. Meanwhile, Dad joined his erstwhile mate and elected to chase after Wolf, running at a speed much greater than the real Dad had ever shown himself capable.

"Well," said Mom, not even out of breath, "I think this one needs her nails clipped, and then a very special bath."

"You mean the liquid that gives ringworm and bald patches?"

asked Dad, dragging Wolf back as though the German shepherd weighed no more than a lapdog.

"And then maybe we'll feed her on hair balls after that," said Mom, shaking Kitnip in her fist.

"I've got plans for this one, too," said Dad, glaring at Wolf. "But we must wait until *he* tells us what he wants. I don't think that was his magic just now."

Mom was surprised. "Wouldn't he take Fay and Clive so he could replace them, like us?"

Dad shook his head: "Then why not take the animals as well? And I thought the real children would be with us for some time yet. Let's play it safe. We'll lock up these two and wait for instructions."

"From the TV?"

Dad was already at the door and gesturing for Mom to follow. "However he decides," was the only reasonable answer. Wolf and Kitnip were unceremoniously dragged into the house and tossed in the basement.

The room disappeared. Fay had been looking down toward her sneakers when she opened the letter. The first thing she saw was brightly colored stone under her feet. And she was standing at a slight tilt. She almost lost her balance but Clive caught her.

Clive had been looking at a picture of the Gurney family from happier days, hanging on the wall over by Dad's broken CD player. (Dad had commented bitterly that if he'd been more interested in the other kind of CD, the kind that meant Certificate of Deposit, they wouldn't be in the mess they were in now.)

When the picture vanished, Clive saw a gigantic marble statue of a man standing in the distance. It was too far away for him to make out the features but close enough to recognize its martial aspect; the figure held a sword pointed straight over its head.

"Where are we?" asked Clive.

"Grandfather wasn't kidding about his powers," whispered Fay.

They took inventory of their new situation for which task they were well situated, high atop a gigantic mound of stone. It was big enough to be considered a mountain but its smoothness suggested a hill. Wherever they were, it seemed to be midday and visibility was excellent under a startlingly blue sky. The only other time Clive could remember a sky like that had been when his parents had taken him to see some historic mining town in Colorado when Fay was only a kid.

Fay was first to see the volcano. It was about the same distance away as the statue but down another quarter of the circle as they turned slowly around. Everywhere they looked there were marvels, but the volcano belonged in a class by itself because of what it was doing: erupting in complete silence.

And yet it had a more arresting feature. The contents of the eruption were not rocks and lava but giant bubbles with bright lights shining inside. These objects rose to a point directly above the mountain before exploding (also silently). They made flashes of light as they disappeared.

"Everything Grandfather told us was true!" Clive sounded miserable.

"No, you mustn't think that," answered Fay quickly. "I will never believe anything he said about Mom and Dad, no matter how much magic he has now."

"You didn't believe he had any magic the day he told us!"

"You didn't either!"

Fay could usually talk herself out of a bad mood. Clive envied her this ability; but when she got herself all worked up, she could carry her brother along with her. This was no time to bicker, with the world they knew vanished only minutes before.

They took in their surroundings as slowly and carefully as if one sudden movement might shatter this strange world, or themselves, into a million pieces. They were at the very apex of the smooth hill of stone, a hill descending so gradually that it looked perfectly safe to traverse.

The hill was four different colors, each making up one quarter of the circle. At first glance, these sections appeared to be painted, but the shades were natural to the rock, even though they were separated by perfectly straight lines. Fay straddled green and yellow. Clive was off to her side, completely in a zone that was red. The remaining color was pure white.

At the axis where the lines met was an ornate telescope, covered in gold and silver bricabrac, and appearing to be something out of a Jules Verne book. Its base was firmly anchored in the rock itself at the exact center of the stone mountain.

Clive looked through the telescope first. It was pointed at the statue. He couldn't believe what he saw, but it made a kind of demented sense. "You gotta see this," he insisted, gesturing to Fay.

She did ... and found herself gazing on the stern, solemn, angry face of Grandfather, chiseled out of a great amount of white marble! Back home, he would have considered such a statement of vanity to be more money that it was worth, no matter the choice of subject.

The telescope could be turned a full 360 degrees for the whole tour. Clive decided to let Fay take the first turn. He was shaken by the face on the statue, and although he wouldn't admit it to her, he felt his sister was probably more qualified than he to understand the unbelievable. After all, she'd had the dreams.

Quite a lot could be seen with the naked eye, but for the few landmarks to be studied, the telescope was indispensable. Each color extended beyond the hill to a vast plateau below. The hill was ringed by trees, and these spread out to make a great forest. Where the white section ended, the trees were covered in snow and ice, except for the ones that stood up like grey splinters, dead husks with naked branches. The only place with snow was the white section.

The red section led into a part of the very strange forest where the trees had leaves of many different shapes and sizes, as well as dozens of colors. They were gold and red and orange and brown, and all kinds of combinations. Some of these leaves were falling from the branches but no sooner did one go than it was replaced by a new leaf, usually of a different color.

The remainder of the woods was marked off where the green and yellow sections ended. Here the trees were covered in bright, green leaves. There were birds singing and chirping in the branches. They sounded like normal birds — at least the kind of birds one might notice back home.

Fay studied a small river dividing the two sections, but from this distance at least, there didn't seem to be much different about these two areas of woodland. Once she got over the surprise of the segregated sections, where different kinds of weather were cut off from each other as by a force field, she was most fascinated by the large objects dominating the horizon. For this task, the telescope was indispensable.

The giant statue stood where the white woods ended. The volcano marked the end of the green section. As for the other two, the red section was watched over by what could only be described as a titanic totem pole. With the aid of the telescope, Fay could make out details of exquisite birds and animals, and human faces, up and down the length of a column of wood that must be nearly two hundred feet high and yards wide! At the base of the column there was an ornate Victorian house, with a door made of the same wood as the pole, and covered in carvings as well.

But an object even stranger than the volcano dominated the yellow section: it appeared to be a giant glass cocoon, or beehive, reflecting its surroundings back at the viewer instead of being transparent. The absence of any knob or adjustability to the eyepiece frustrated Fay. The range of the telescope was too limited to satisfy her curiosity. Beyond the large objects on the horizon, there was very little she could make out. There was a yellow fog hanging over much of the landscape past that point.

She had seen that fog before.

"Here, Clive," she said, appreciating how smoothly the telescope swiveled on its mount. He was ready now and eagerly lowered his face to the eyepiece. Yet none of the oddities she had witnessed compared to the most remarkable aspect of the place. More than anything else, what proved to Fay that she was no longer on Earth was the absence of the sun! Which left the problem: where did the light originate?

Nothing cast any shadows under the empty, blue sky. That took a bit of getting used to. She tapped Clive on the shoulder and let him in on her latest discovery. He didn't believe her at first, but the matter was quickly settled when she asked him about the light. She was just about to conclude that her brother was being dense (one of her bad habits) when he came through like gangbusters.

"Do you suppose," he began earnestly, "that the bubbles from the volcano provide the light? They look like little suns when they pop."

Suddenly they felt a wind, and with it came the sound of chimes. Fay began to shake, but the wind was warm and pleasant. She had a terrible thought: if Grandfather had come here after he died, did this mean that they were dead, too? Did this place have a name they weren't supposed to say in school? Even though she was younger, she often felt older than her brother. She decided to keep this idea to herself.

Fay bent down and picked up the envelope. When the blackness first poured out, she'd felt paper inside. Now seemed a good time to double-check. Sure enough, there were two pages inside. The first was hand written with a flowing penmanship that was beautiful and as easy to read as if it had been typed.

"What does it say?" asked Clive.

She read it aloud to him. She was a good reader.

Dear Fay and Clive,

Please forgive the unorthodox method by which I have reached you. If you are reading this page, then the transition has already taken place. You are on the Mound of Seasons, the center of a shrinking dimension. The fate of your world is tied to what happens here, as are millions of other worlds.

Malak is reborn from a member of your family, and he has stolen your parents because he needs them for a sacrifice when the moment is right. There is no walking away from the blood, dear ones. You are tied to them and tied to him; on your heads falls the fate of more than I can possibly relate in a letter.

He Who Was Your Grandfather and is now Malak, the Dour One, is at war with the Seasons. He hates them all, even Winter, although he once pretended to prefer it, and now has his fortress there. Most of all he hates Summer which is why he chose this time of your year for the attack.

As Fay read and Clive listened, they were both too intent on the matter at hand to notice a subtle change in the color of the white statue dominating the Winter region. The sword was darkening, and as this happened, a wind started up and blew at the young Gurneys. This was no ordinary wind but came in a narrow shaft of air, as if an arrow had been loosed at them.

Your parents were replaced with creatures called Slaks. Eventually he would have replaced you, as well, but not until you had performed certain tasks for him on earth. By bringing you here ahead of schedule, we've caused him a problem and given you a chance. The most important thing is that you should come to me at my house; it is the only house in the Land of the Seasons, and you can see it at the far end of Autumn by using the telescope you will find waiting for you. I cannot come to you because....

Fay would have read more but at that moment the shaft of wind struck. It was the coldest wind Fay had ever felt, but it just grazed the tips of her fingers, discoloring them with a blue-grey frost. She didn't let go of the letter. The words on the page changed color, from their original black to grey and then a white that could barely be discerned, before falling to shatter into a thousand shards against the hard rock surface below. The last two words to fall were: *Mrs. Norse.*

"I want out of here," said Clive.

Fay screamed once. "Oh, what are we going to do now?" she moaned, and started shaking. Clive put his arm around her and tried to let his mind go as blank as the sheet of paper in her hand.

"Wait," he had the presence of mind to say, "check the other page."

It had not been affected, but it was no communication from Mrs. Norse. It was a love poem Dad had written to Mom the first year of their marriage:

"Honey, I don't pretend that this rhymes or scans, but I passed poetry in college and this is the best I can do."

To My Girl

When the end of the rainbow leads not to pots of gold,
Other treasures may fill to vaulted ceilings a woman's soul;
If worldly woes squeeze today's happiness from an open heart
still dreams of hope replenish passion from old love's dart.
The world is too much with us, eroding lives with distance,
Life becomes an aching trap when beauty forgets its radiance;
We long for Eden before the Fall, sin untasted on the tree,
You are all that ever matters, more than words could ever be.
Oh, to grind our fears to bread on which to feed laughter
So that tribulations are food as we are happy forever after!
Good faith is man's aspiration and woman's armor, her sheen,
For in the end, happy memories are all a prince of fools may
set before his Queen.

Fay read it. Clive wore a critic's expression throughout the experience. "I wonder why Mrs. Norse sent us this," she said.

"I wonder why it wasn't messed up by the wind, too," he said with a touch of regret. "We better do what Mrs. Norse said. At least we got that much from the letter." He held out his hand to help, expecting her to favor her weakened ankle.

"Clive!" she cried out. "I didn't notice until now. There's been so much happening. My ankle is fine. It's like I never sprained it!"

Chapter Six
Wolf And Kitnip

"That's great news, sis," said Clive. "It should be easier for you to get down. This is what I've always wanted, a real adventure."

"Oh Clive, grow up," said his younger sister. "This isn't a game."

"I didn't say it was, but it does sort of look like one from up here."

"Clive!" She could sound just like her mother when she was upset. "I'm afraid."

"I know. I am, too. God, I hate Granddad." Just mentioning their nemesis made the day — if they could call the endless blue sky a day — seem all the heavier. "You know, what are we going to call him from now on? It's getting ridiculous calling him ... you know."

With a wistful smile, Fay remembered how the man didn't like them addressing him by anything less formal than Grandfather. "The Mrs. Norse lady has given us enough names to choose from."

"Malak," whispered Clive.

"The Dour One," echoed Fay. They might have gone on in this vein a while longer except that they were distracted by the presence of a cloud. It wouldn't have been worth noting back home ... but as the first cloud they had seen here, it was quite an event. They hadn't noticed it forming over the distant sword of the statue shortly after they lost the Norse letter.

The cloud moved very fast. As it grew nearer, it became darker. Clive had seen a tornado once at summer camp. It hadn't been very large, but was big enough to be a killer. The tornado was the most scared Clive had ever been. Until now.

The cloud was funnelling down, taking on the resemblance of that long-ago windstorm.

"We've got to get away from here!" Clive shouted over the wind, but his advice wasn't necessary. The tip of the funnel struck the rock near them, and began a zig-zag movement in their direction. They held hands but it didn't do any good. Before the funnel reached them, they were torn apart by the surging wind. Clive went tumbling down the red path, while Fay was forced back along the yellow.

For one insane moment the funnel lifted straight over Fay's head. She expected to be pulled up inside it and torn to pieces. She could see the dark tunnel of wind, lit by flashing electricity as little tornadoes bounced back and forth along the inside of the walls. Then it moved on, leaving her both awestruck and alive.

The tornado continued in a straight line away from her, but other winds came behind it. She could see Clive disappearing over the rise and called out, but the wind drowned out her voice. The blank sheet that had been Mrs. Norse's letter went fluttering off in the direction of the giant statue but she held on to her father's poem and jammed it back in the envelope, shoving it in the side pocket of her shorts. While she was saving the paper, her glasses fell off and smashed against the rock.

Then she made a mistake. Reaching for her glasses after it was too late made her fall. She started rolling painfully down the hill. The distance from the stone hill to the ground was over a thousand feet, and if she didn't stop tumbling very soon, she could be killed by the unyielding granite surface. Fortunately, it wasn't very steep, and a respite in the wind allowed her the opportunity to stand.

She attempted to work her way back up to the top so she could find Clive, but when she tried, the wind started up again, pressing down on her with sudden force, as if an invisible wall opposed her. There was no choice but to continue toward the ground below.

The yellow rock under her feet gradually turned to pebbles,

and before she knew it, she was safely walking on green grass. The moment the hill was left behind, the air changed. There was a pleasant cool breeze, nothing like the freak storm she'd left behind. Other than that, the day was warm, but not hot. She looked up, expecting to see the sun, but, of course, it wasn't there. She had no idea where the warmth was coming from.

When she could accept the fact that she was safe, her legs gave out and she gratefully collapsed on the soft grass. She allowed herself the luxury of crying. This was not a good day.

Gradually her vision cleared as she wiped the tears away, and she took deep breaths, half choking because she was so upset. She began examining the red scrapes on her knees and elbows, and some purple bruises as bad as what Clive had gotten from his father. She was all set to cry again when she realized that she'd received another gift besides her improved ankle (which had miraculously survived its undignified descent down the hill). Her various injuries were vivid and clear to her eye. Unconsciously, she reached up to adjust her glasses.

That's when she remembered she'd lost her glasses. Her vision had been restored to a perfect 20/20. Somehow this dried up her reserve supply of tears. She got to her feet and turned around to check out the stone mountain. She was only a few feet from it. There was a crazy slanting effect, as her perspective shifted. She had to close her eyes for a moment, but she still saw the yellow under the lids, from all that yellow on her side of the hill.

A few years ago, the family had been able to afford their last real vacation. They'd done the whole Florida bit, from Disney World to Sea World to Cape Kennedy. When they'd gone to see the Vehicle Assembly Building, she'd pressed her nose right up against the side of the biggest building — by square foot volume — in the world. She'd thought the side of the building was moving, crushing down on her, as the sheer bulk of what she saw was too much for the brain to register. What was happening to her now was like that, but different; more a case of the side of the mountain sliding sideways under her gaze than looming over her.

She sat down on the ground a second time. There was no medication if she should have another headache. Taking deep, regular breaths to calm herself, she knew this was a time for thinking things through. Her dreams had never suggested there might be a place like this for real, except that there were differences. She'd seen nothing like the floating cages yet. But the yellow fog was all too familiar.

First of all, she realized the visual anomaly she'd just experienced had to do with her eyes adjusting to their new strength. Despite all the miracles that had occurred, the hill wasn't really moving. Tentatively, she turned her head and took another look at the yellow side of the mountain. It was fine now. Except that it did seem bigger somehow. From where she was sitting, she couldn't see an end to the yellow on either side.

The question was what to do next? Before they were attacked by the mysterious cloud, they had decided to go visit the lady who brought them here. By bad luck, Fay was not in the right location. The last she had seen of her brother, he was going down the red section, the correct section.

She decided it was time to keep calm by talking things over with herself. "You need to get to the red section where Mrs. Norse is," she told herself and the universe at large. It was reasonable to assume that Clive would head for the house; but since when did reason have anything to do with a brother's actions? He might even now be trying to find her, a far more impossible task than doing Mrs. Norse's bidding. There was no avoiding the troublesome matter of reunion. An obvious first step had to be taken.

She stood up, faced the hill and called out Clive's name as loudly as she could, waiting about thirty seconds between shouts. After five tries, with not even an echo to keep her company, she gave up. There was no point in losing her voice.

Next she marched straight up to the hill with a plan to follow it around until she reached the end of this section of forest. Even if the hill seemed bigger, it would only take so long to get where she was going. She was sorry she'd left her Batman watch at home. Suddenly she laughed, as she remembered the absence of the sun. Here she was thinking about seconds and minutes and hours in a world that had no way of measuring time! She wondered if Clive had brought his watch. She hadn't noticed when they were on the hill.

At any rate, she had more serious problems to worry about, such as deciding whether she should go to the right or the left. She tried to remember how the colors had been laid out. It had been green, yellow, red and white. Choose the correct direction and the very next section of woods would be the right one.

She started following the edge of the hill, moving to her left. "That's a bad choice," whispered a soft voice from behind. She whirled around, but didn't see anyone. "I'm down here," the voice spoke again.

Lowering her eyes, just a bit nervously, she saw a familiar face licking a paw, and rubbing its head. Kitnip! For the first time in her life, Fay had absolutely nothing to say.

"You were thinking of trying to get to Mrs. Norse's woods that way, weren't you?" asked the cat, infernally calm.

Fay used all her will power and produced one hesitant word: "Kitnip?"

"I never liked that name. Made me sound like a drug addict, just waiting for my next whiff of the old catnip. Or else the name made me sound too cute for words."

"But how...?"

"You want to know how I'm here. Fair enough, but there's no time for that now. If Wolf and I hadn't been rescued shortly after you left, we'd be in that great pound in the sky by now."

"But how...?"

"If you weren't such a smart girl, I'd think you're repeating yourself. But we know better, don't we? You want to know how it is that I talk."

"Yes."

"No time for that either. Sorry!" Whereupon Kitnip had the nerve to rub up against her leg and purr. "Now let's go, but not to Autumn. Since we're already in Spring, our best choice is to make for the Hive. We must get there as soon as possible."

"While it's still daylight?"

"I have the distinct impression that there's no night here," said the cat, "but I suppose I could be wrong. I'll miss the night."

Fay had to admit the cat seemed to recognize the implications of their environment better than she did. She would like to have discussed the matter but Kitnip had other ideas. When a cat decides to really move, it is a challenge to keep up. In addition, Fay was exhausted from everything that had happened to her in one day. Kitnip darted off into the woods so quickly that Fay was lost before she started. "Kitnip," she cried out. "Don't leave me!"

Just as quickly as she disappeared, Kitnip returned, standing on a tree stump with her tail forming a curlicue, like a question mark. The cat turned her head sideways as she said, "Sorry. You can't help it that you're physically challenged, what with only having two legs."

"Please don't rub it in. How much time do we have, assuming there is such a thing as time here. I don't see how you'd measure it."

"You humans make up a way of telling time no matter where you are, so don't worry about it. There are two conditions: moving and standing still. Let's get moving."

"It's just that I'm so tired," Fay admitted reluctantly. "If I could only rest..."

The cat purred — or was it a hmmmmmm? — before she relented: "We can let you take a nap, but only for what you'd call an hour. You know, the way you've been acting lately, I'm worried you're narcoleptic or something."

Moving with great deliberation, Kitnip led Fay to a stand of pine trees. Fay loved their smell, and these were very large and beautiful. Underfoot it became thick with pine needles, and there were only a few pine cones to be kicked out of the way. She approved of Kitnip's choice of bed for her.

"I'll feel better after just a little bit," said Fay, lying down on the soft pine needles, enjoying the feel of the hard ground underneath. In one day she would have gone to sleep outdoors twice, once with Wolf as her companion and now with Kitnip. But was she really in the same day, or wasn't that a universe ago? She didn't want to think about it.

Wondering idly how Kitnip had arrived (surely a cat didn't receive mail), the last thing she saw was a patch of blue sky overhead, with limbs of the trees gently swaying against it; and the pine cones up high were black dots like so many eyes gazing down.

Clive landed dead center in a pile of autumn leaves that probably saved him from serious injury. He didn't feel very grateful, perhaps because there was something else in the leaves, something under him that started reaching up, under his pants leg, with spidery, cold fingers.

Yelping, Clive bolted out of the leaves and started running. He didn't really want to know what was behind him, but boys will be boys. Stealing a glance inspired him to run all the harder.

The pursuer was four feet high and seemed to be made out of both vegetable and metal parts. The head had the appearance of a crazy jack-'o-lantern. The eyes were black holes, but something red swum inside. The mouth had teeth. The whole body moved like a machine with three legs, the middle one pushing over and over again like a piston. And the absolute worst thing about it was that it called out Clive's name in a screaming falsetto.

Clive had seen more than enough. There was nothing else to do but concentrate on serious running. He was going so fast that he didn't notice the second one until he'd tripped over it. This one was only three feet tall, but it was bigger because it was longer. It had eight legs, like a spider, and they were all metal, but the main part of the body seemed to be made of the same vegetable substance as the other one's head. There was one stalk growing out of the center, and at its tip blinked an eye, which took this opportunity to slowly swivel around and consider one frightened human being.

This time Clive didn't feel like he was running; he was flying. He had to get away from these monsters! Every sound he heard conjured up images of even more terrible things coming from behind. Maybe they didn't climb trees, he thought. Maybe he should get off the ground. There was a big oak just up ahead, and it had a limb low down over the ground, in easy reaching distance which he grabbed without losing his stride. He hoisted himself into the air.

Unfortunately, he wasn't holding on to a part of the tree. Instead, another of the creatures held on to him. It was elongated like a snake and didn't seem to have any metal parts. It was all of one color, and so dark that one didn't recognize the shade as a kind of orange until one was up against it. The way Clive happened to be right now!

Falling to the ground, with the thing coiling around his body, Clive had the air knocked out of him. He was too stunned to do much about it but look dazedly at the head of the monster peering into his eyes. There was a human face, but all shriveled and withered, like a shrunken head.

When he heard the rustling of leaves behind him, he assumed it was more of them coming to finish him off. He wondered what it would be like to die. His only regret was that he wouldn't be around to help Fay find their real Mom and Dad. He was very sorry about that. He even felt sorry for his father for the first time since the beating. If Clive were about to die, he wanted to forgive Dad while there was still time.

Suddenly, there was a loud barking just behind his head. The thing holding him unwrapped itself and slithered away. As he started to get up, he saw another of the creatures moving off to the side. There were a half dozen of them. The sight of the spider thing literally running up a tree made him sick to his stomach.

The barking repeated itself, louder and closer than before. The last of the creatures scurried out of sight. Clive couldn't believe his ears, so he trusted to sight instead.

Sure enough, Wolf was standing next to him, guarding Clive with a ferocity he'd never seen in the dog before. With one last growl, Wolf ignored the enemy, and raised his head to look Clive squarely in the face.

"I got here just in time," said the dog.

"It's you, boy, but how can you talk?"

"I've always talked, you just never understood before. And I don't like being called 'boy' anymore than you do."

Clive didn't know what surprised him more — that his dog talked, or that he had an attitude. "But how did you get here?" he asked.

"I couldn't begin to explain, but I know what we have to do. We've got to reach the house before this invasion is over. Come on." And with that, the dog started running; but he had gone less than one yard, before he stopped and looked back, to make sure that Clive was following.

Clive didn't feel very well after what he'd gone through, but he could sense the urgency and forced himself to run hard, ignoring the pain. He was amazed about many things, not least of which was that the monsters seemed to be afraid of his dog. This knowledge gave him confidence to carry on.

He was glad for Wolf's aid, when suddenly the dog disappeared behind a mound of earth, covered in moss. For a brief instant of alarm, Clive sympathized with all the times he'd deliberately lost Fay when she was following him in the woods. Younger sisters will follow big brothers, no matter how annoying that might be.

He debated with himself over whether or not he should call out Wolf's name — he laughed out loud when he realized that if Wolf said his own name it would sound like: "Woof"! Suddenly the decision was taken out of his hands. The dog returned, heading straight for him.

"Hide," Wolf commanded. After the bravery the dog had shown, this could be no idle advice. Something really dangerous must be moving in their direction.

The two of them went behind the bole of a huge tree (it looked like a redwood) when the subject of Wolf's consternation strode into the small clearing. It was Malak, the Dour One. It was Grandfather.

Chapter Seven
Dour Sendings

Fay woke up. She had been having a lovely dream about her family at the seashore. This was the first pleasant dream she'd had in months. But when she awakened, it was to another nightmare.

It was the same view of the pine trees waving gently against the blue sky, only something new had been added. At first she thought she was looking at the moon, but a round, pale face intruded into her halcyon dream of peace. Or could it really be called a face, when it was a pure white human skull? As it turned slightly, she saw an envelope of nearly transparent flesh around it, the clear, jelly-like substance that glistens on a jellyfish. A moment later, the whole body came into view and Fay did the only reasonable thing.

She screamed. Then she screamed again. The figure ran away, and she heard Kitnip's voice scolding her: "You scared him away."

"I scared *him?*" she asked incredulously. Then she completely forgot herself, where she was, and with whom she was dealing. She blurted out: "You let that creature sneak up on me!"

"Calm down," purred Kitnip. "I should have warned you about their appearances, but it just so happens that Tabriks are friends. They live in the glass hive."

Fay screwed up her face, the way she always did when she was worrying. Kitnip could hardly believe how nasty her friend was becoming, especially when Fay launched into a tirade: "So now you're telling me that I'm to blame if we have problems with these bone people, or whatever they are. How could I possibly know..."

"Humans," commented Kitnip with a weariness that could only come from having experienced them for more than one lifetime. "You simply must calm down or I'll leave."

Now that was a surprise. She didn't have the slightest idea how the cat had come to be here, but she just naturally assumed they would have the same purposes. As far as dealing with an animal, she had always prided herself on treating her pets with respect. But it was a very different matter when another mind suddenly came into the picture ... and in such an unlikely package, too!

Fay was mad. She wanted to tell Kitnip to go live with the Tabriks if that's the way she felt about it. But Fay didn't need a lesson more than once, in which respect she was different from her brother. In her most formal tone she gravely addressed her former pet: "I believe I owe you an apology."

Kitnip rubbed up against her leg and purred. She might suddenly be another person with an active mind but she was still a cat as well. Fay relaxed, and started scratching the cat on the head, and gently crushing the ears the way she liked.

"All right, then" said the cat. "We need to be moving on. I'm sure we can find the Tabriks before there's trouble. Now there's one thing about being courteous to Tabriks, besides not screaming when you see one. No human being can possibly pronounce their personal names, so it's better you don't even try. I found that out when I first arrived."

"Can you do it?" asked Fay.

"No. Mrs. Norse brought me down in the middle of a party she was having for some of them and I didn't have a mouse's chance of making a good impression. But enough chatter. Let's go!"

Whether Fay was rested or not, she liked the idea of moving. In a place where the creature she had just seen wasn't to be feared, she hated to think what something really scary might be like. Besides, she really did feel better after her nap.

"Before we go any further, we need to take something along for our protection," said the cat. "You need to collect those pine cones."

Now that was a strange request! There were about half a dozen cones scattered about, considerably less than might have expected from so many trees. Fay was learning not to question her unexpected benefactor — at least not all at once. But there was a practical difficulty.

"I hate to bring this up, Kitnip, but I don't have anything to carry them in. I left my knapsack at home."

"Yeah, I remember. It's the red one made of Goretex. I guess you'll have to take your top off and make a bag to carry them in."

The funny thing wasn't that Fay felt a sudden hesitation, down deep in her stomach, but that she could be embarrassed in front of Kitnip. They were just girls here. Her cat had seen her with no clothes on plenty of times. She used to take Kitnip into the bathroom with her when she would take a bath and the cat would get on the closed toilet seat and peer over into the water. When using bubble bath, it was especially funny because the cat would make batting motions at the bubbles, and when the suds would get on her paw, she'd hold it up in front of her, as if inspecting a trophy.

Well, it was one thing to have no modesty with a pet and quite another with a brand new person! Even if that person didn't happen to be human. Kitnip wasn't hers anymore. Then again, cat people were always saying how easily they accepted the idea that nobody owns a cat. The quickest way to test that proposition would be to have their pets express an opinion.

This was getting nowhere fast. Why shouldn't she take off her top? It was a warm day. Mother had tried to teach Fay to be modest about wearing tops back when her chest was completely flat, and she couldn't see why she couldn't have the same freedom outdoors that Clive had. When the first small bumps came, she realized that Mom had wanted her to practice. This was apparently what women did. They practiced a lot.

Well, this was a different world, and maybe it had different rules. She'd already stopped thinking it might be Hell. But there was plenty of proof that it wasn't Heaven either. Maybe all worlds you could travel to, in your own body, were mixtures of good and bad.

"OK," she said, and removed the top, noticing only for the briefest moment the current status of her breasts. At least they were starting to be something. They reminded her of the pointy tips of inverted ice cream cones. That's what Uncle Celko called them anyway. She thought of them more as Hershey kisses. She hoped that one day they would be as full and round as Mom's.

"I don't suppose you'll tell me why we need pine cones," she said a bit sarcastically as she began to gather them.

"I don't mind. In the hands of humans, they can be deadly explosives..."

"What?!"

"... if thrown against the right targets. We're in Spring, and there are protections against Malak here. His agents fear what the Tabriks have placed throughout this Season to thwart him. Autumn has Mrs. Norse to protect it, but as she is his greatest enemy, he is bringing most of his forces to bear against her. Summer is the most vulnerable."

"How do you know all this? You told me there wasn't time before, but..."

"It's very complicated to tell, but simple to show. When we have reached the Hive, you'll have all the answers you can bear." The cat made the proposition sound downright grizzly.

She would have asked Kitnip what sort of dangers they might face on the journey, but thought better of it. At least it was a relief to learn they were in one of the safer areas. Even so, the cat was right to observe caution if Malak could strike against them anywhere.

Malak. Grandfather. It was hard to believe they were the same person. She hadn't heard the cat admit to this knowledge. Come to think of it, Kitnip would have only seen her grandparent on rare occasions. The family had never been close, just another of its many problems.

This was no time to explore the subject. Kitnip was moving off, more slowly this time, and Fay was grateful that her feline friend was pacing herself to be more easily followed. Making a knot at the top of her shirt, Fay proudly noticed that none of the cones fell out when she lifted her makeshift bag. She doubted any snooty girl scout could do better.

It was good to be on the move again, now that she had rested. And good not to have to think too much about what had happened to Mom, Dad ... and Clive!

"My dear boy," said the old man who was Malak, the Dour One, and who just happened to be Clive's grandfather. "I can smell you hiding there. Sort of like 'Fee, Fi, Fo, Fum' in the old fairy tale. You can't hide Gurney blood from me!"

Clive started shaking. Wolf growled, way down low, but you could still hear it. Grandfather didn't miss a beat: "So you have that old mongrel with you, too. You never took good care of the beast. But then you never bathed yourself very well either, which is why I can find you now. There's nothing preventing me sending my little friends right up to you and having them eat out your eyeballs."

Clive whimpered. Wolf growled in words: "I've had just about enough."

"Fear not, Clive. Sheath your fangs, Wolf. I'll not attack you today. If you have one good brain between the two of you, then you'll recognize the folly of attacking when I am surrounded by my autumnal legions."

"What do you want?" demanded Wolf, and his voice was different, full of fire and thunder every bit as frightening as the unbearable confidence of their enemy.

"Fair enough. I want what I always want: a bargain." He allowed silence to collect in the air, and then it sort of drifted down to different parts of their bodies, touching Clive's fingers and ears, pressing up against Wolf's nose. The longer it went on, the worst it got until finally Wolf's impatience was stronger than Clive's fear.

"Stay there," said Wolf, and padded out from behind the tree so that the Dour One could see him. "We're not buying anything today," said the dog.

"Good," came the reply, "because I'm not selling."

The parley was fairly begun. "So what's this about?" Wolf wanted to know.

"I'm buying. What would you say to a once-in-a-lifetime bargain? You have something I want to invest in. Now ask yourself, what is the best possible investment?"

Wolf had a ready answer: "A bone."

The Dour One was well named. Anyone else might have at least cracked a smile at the canine thought. But Grandfather had never laughed at jokes. He didn't even seem to hear what anyone else said, but continued on his solitary course.

"The best investment is something that can never go wrong, that always pays and pays and pays. Many wise people have given this problem much thought over the centuries and they always arrive at the same answer. The best investment is taxes. The power to collect them is the only security in the universe. The best stocks are the ones you put slaves in. Why create anything if you can force others to satisfy your needs? "

Clive listened to the dry, cold voice. Although he didn't understand the exact meaning of much of what the old man said, the general idea was simple enough. Granddad was not a nice man.

"What has any of this to do with us?" asked the dog.

"I'm offering the two of you employment," he answered solemnly. "Join my friendly army of tax collectors! There's a big project coming up and it will take a lot to pull it off. Now we don't use regular money around here. We pay for what we want in more ineffable substances, but I'll teach you what they are and how to get them."

Even though Wolf had told him to stay put, Clive came out from behind the tree. He'd understood enough of what Grandfather was saying that he had to show himself and say something.

"But Grandfather..." Clive began.

"Ah, my dear, sweet boy!" said the man.

"Granddad!" Clive tried again to seize the other's attention, and half expected to be called down for using the name he'd been told to avoid ... but nothing happened. "Why do you want us?"

"Why not?"

"Didn't you have a task for us back on earth?"

The man allowed himself the briefest of smiles as if to say: Clive is using strategy! Now who would have expected that? Grandfather bowed in honor of the indirect approach and explained, "A certain terrible lady altered my plans, but we shouldn't cry over the spilled milk of kindness. I'm in a magnanimous mood and offer you this splendid opportunity with job security and automatic promotions."

Clive wasn't in a buying or selling mood: "But back on Earth, you were always cursing the IRS. You had nothing good to say about taxes."

"That is true," said the man.

"Then what's this about?" asked Wolf.

"There is an important difference, you two." Grandfather started to grin. He grinned so broadly that he looked like a happy man. Clive had never seen that before. Grandfather also looked younger. "The difference is that here I collect the taxes," said He Who Was Malak. "Back there, I had to give them."

"You didn't really mean it when you complained to Mom and Dad every April?"

"To anyone who would listen!" Grandfather helpfully finished the thought. "I was very bitter about anyone taking my money. The operative word is mine! There's no reason you should know about my poor business partner, Larry. We had diversified into computers at just the right time. He railed against the government more than anyone I've ever met. The poor fool thought I agreed with him on principle every time I was merely practical. When we received an offer that would mean upgrading the IRS computers, he wanted to turn it down. A contract worth millions. Poor old Larry. I had to get rid of him."

"You ... killed him?" Clive dared to ask.

Now the man laughed. Grandfather had never done that, never! Who was this strange amalgam of at least two different people, Lord Malak with Grandfather's mind and sordid memories?

"You never have to murder idealists, boy. You can take care of them legally. That's what the law is for, to reward practical people."

As Malak elaborated the point, the weird creatures that so terrified the boy wandered into the clearing and surrounded their leader. Clive had no idea there were so many. He counted a dozen in plain view, and the movement of bushes suggested there were many, many more.

Suddenly Wolf broke the spell. "We don't want to touch your money, or what you use for it."

Their would-be employer was most forgiving: "Ah, you wouldn't know real money from Kibbels and Bits. Besides, we're not talking about money in the way you mean. Everything runs on magic hereabouts. I need more magic in one place at one time than has ever happened since Creation, little pooch. I started the ball rolling with the spell I chanted on Pine Lake back on earth a lifetime ago. You might say that was my audition. Now I have the best job there is, and I'm offering you a little piece of action instead of the alternative."

Clive was finding it hard to breathe for some reason. It was as if every spoken word was hitting him in the chest. Most annoying was that he felt like crying from that little balloon that fills up deep inside with all the tears you try never to show. He couldn't stand to listen to anymore.

"Where's Dad?" he blurted out.

"You're changing the subject," said Malak.

Clive's answer flowed out of him like a river of pain: "You used to say you hated Dad because he couldn't make enough money. But if you want all the money for yourself, then you'd hate Dad for making money, too."

"The innocent babe has spoken a Truth," said the very old man who looked far too young.

"You'd hate him either way!" Clive could hardly believe what he heard himself saying. Wolf observed the boy with sympathy, but in this situation, there was nothing he could do for him.

"I hate you!" shouted Clive at the figure standing before him, the monster who had once been part of his family.

"There's no percentage in that," said the Dour One. "I'll give you one more chance."

"We've heard enough from you," said Wolf as he started backing away until he was right up against Clive. That's when Grandfather gave them a taste of the alternative: he pulled off his head and threw it at them.

Chapter Eight
Crookies

Meanwhile, back in the world so recently departed....

Aunt Miner decided to pay a surprise visit on her favorite relatives, which unfortunates turned out to be the Gurneys, as usual. Only this time, Aunt Miner would be the one who received a surprise.

The woman had an uncanny knack for making promises that never came true. It was often suggested that she take up a career as a family counselor, or failing that try her hand in one of the banking professions. If she said that you could count on something absolutely, then you could be certain of the opposite. One of her many promises was that she'd never drop in unannounced.

The funny thing about the situation was that it turned out to be the best visit Aunt Miner ever had with the Gurneys. First of all, she never got along terribly well with children. She would accept any plausible excuse to explain their absence. For her, the make-believe Mom and Dad were perfectly convincing, and perfect in every other way.

"Clive and Fay are visiting friends," said Dad with a big smile.

"Friends they met at school," added Mom with a bigger smile.

Aunt Miner rarely listened to anyone but she could give the appearance of engaging in conversation. What they had already told her was more than sufficient to satisfy her curiosity (weak at the best of times); but she stuck to the topic, out of a feeling that parents are interested in their children, even if no one else is.

And so she asked, "Are they spending their whole summer vacation with these children?" Hers was an indifferent inquiry, raised in the hope that perhaps the absence of the children would mean a longer visit from everyone's favorite aunt.

The man who looked just like Dad said, "Yes."

The woman who looked just like Mom said, "No." Unfortunately, they spoke at the same instant. For anyone else in all possible universes this might have been taken as a clue that something was wrong. If Aunt Miner had been paying just a little attention, she might have noticed that the Gurneys were acting like characters out of the TV sitcoms that she so frequently watched.

The point is that Aunt Miner couldn't be allowed to leave and alert someone if she suspected anything. Malak could replace her with a duplicate if he thought someone might miss her (as unlikely as that might be), but it was a decision for him. Basically, the fake Mom and Dad would have to contact the boss.

They couldn't know that poor Aunt Miner wasn't worth plotting against. She wouldn't be a threat to the Dour One's plans if she saw the children whisked away right before supper.

Aunt Miner rambled on in her characteristic way, so that even the cold, calculating minds listening to her every word lost track of what she was saying. One minute she was reminding them that they'd never visited Cousin Orson as they had promised they would before their financial problems. The next second she was complaining about how their carpet wasn't the best material by a long shot, and that its shade clashed with a set of Peruvian ashtrays she had given them.

"... and just where are those ashtrays?" she wanted to know. The fact that the Gurneys had given up smoking around the time of Fay's birth was supremely unimportant to Aunt Miner. She smoked, after all, and ashtrays were a fine gift to provide relations who might be visited by the most loving member of their extended family.

The strangest thing about this sad woman was that if she rambled on long enough she would make some accurate observations, if only in passing. In a minor key, the woman specialized in unpleasant truths; and she'd never realize that she had crossed an invisible line until long suffering relatives would become so upset that even she couldn't help but recognize what she had done. But this time she would have no cause for embarrassment, and no clue as to the actual content of her remarks. Good old fake Mom and Dad would be cheerful no matter what!

Oddly enough, if the real Gurneys had been there they might have learned more than usual from this particular visit. Especially when Aunt Miner laid it on thick with "Mom": "Oh you dear girl, you've always been emotionally stifled, you know. I blame your mother, God rest her soul, but she didn't encourage you to be yourself. Very few parents do. Now you find it hard to open yourself to others, not even to your own brother ... but then he was a little rascal, wasn't he? Too much like his pop, but you always knew that, didn't you? Well, your dear, sweet man has his hands full when you get stubborn, doesn't he? You dig in your heels and nothing on God's green earth can move you."

"Would you like some coffee?" asked fake Mom with a big smile that would make any normal person worry about arsenic poisoning, but Aunt Miner was protected from worry by invincible ignorance. She was proud of the fact that she'd never had an ulcer. No one had ever tried calculate how many stomach ailments she had generously provided to others.

The offer of refreshments did put her on another track, though. It was time for fake Dad to hear unpleasant truths about himself. They went like this: "But you, Old Fellow" — her nickname for Dad — "you could do with a little more sensitivity, you know. Not big gobs of it, like mashed potatoes the way Joe used to serve them. You remember him, don't you? He's a dentist now. He'd never have married Doris if he'd stuck to that ridiculous idea he could be a painter! Doris is a practical woman with her feet on the ground. Oh, where was I?"

The real Mom and Dad would have viewed the momentary lapse in her attention as unmerited favor from on high. Slaks, on the other hand, could continue nodding and smiling as long as was necessary.

Aunt Miner continued: "Anyway, dear old Fellow, you need to notice that the little woman has moods. She's your rock and you don't appreciate her. Sometimes that rock needs communication, and sometimes it needs to be left alone. Why is it that men can never tell when a woman really needs to be alone? She spends half her time tending to his moods while he pretends he doesn't have any, but she needs to rest occasionally and try to find herself, which is harder for us than it is for you....

"I mean, it's not like you men exactly misplace yourselves. You give us as many headaches as you cure, I'll tell you that right now, the way I told my late, dear husband who had his faults, mind you, I'd never say he was a saint ... although he went to Church a great deal."

She went on in this line for some time until even she ran out of steam, and while taking a longer than usual breath allowed for fake Dad to lean over directly in her line of vision and ask, "Would you like some cookies to go with your coffee?"

Aunt Miner responded to him in the usual way, with a barely perceptible nod (except for a few extra words about watching her diet) and then, before she knew it, had a steaming cup in one hand and a big grey cookie in the other. If she'd bothered to notice, she probably wouldn't have actually bitten into the cookie. It wasn't very appetizing, being one of the Dour One's inventions, concocted of the same substance from which he'd fashioned the copies of Mom and Dad. The Slaks had never eaten of these cookies. If they had, it would raise an interesting question about whether or not such activity was cannibalism. Grandfather was of the opinion that whatever you eat, it's not cannibalism unless you know that you're eating your own kind. He'd thought about lots of unusual things before he became more than human, which was good practice for what he was doing now.

Anyway, Aunt Miner had a very big cookie in her hand and was aware that she'd have to stop talking for a moment if she

wanted to eat it. Mom and Dad leaned forward with keen antici-
pation as Aunt Miner stopped talking, took a deep breath and ...
resumed talking.

The last thing the woman said before she started eating was:
"I miss him, I'm not about to deny it. He was a good husband as
husbands go, but he had his faults. We stayed together in those
days, not like young people today. Not that I'm saying we had
stronger values than your generation; I'm just saying that we
stayed together because that's the way it was then. It's such a
different world now. You're all so serious about everything, and
so impatient. You never wait for things the way we did. Why I
remember...."

A more splendid demonstration of the patience of Malak's creations could not have been devised. They waited and waited and
waited. Finally, when it seemed that Aunt Miner lived on the
dulcet tones of her verbiage alone, she bit into the cookie.

She never had a chance to try the coffee. The poor woman just
sat there, frozen in the chair, her skin taking on the same grey
color as the "cookie." She was frozen into place so quickly that
her grip on the cup didn't loosen, and not a drop was spilled.

They judged her a problem to be dealt with later. Something
to put off for a rainy day, the same way Aunt Miner had put off all
the good deeds she had been promising her long suffering family she would take care of eventually.

But that's another story.

Fay caught her breath as she saw the most beautiful scene of
her young life. Kitnip had brought her to a small clearing. A min-
iature waterfall seemed to sing with gurgling water of different
colors, flowing and bubbling its joyful tune. Cool air rose from
the little pool of sparkling water, carrying a scent of fresh mint
and ice.

A variety of birds darted about, and they were of as many hues as the water. The ones she found most attractive had double-sets of wings, one blue and one black, and when they were flying the wings would move so fast that they would blur, as if the wings of hummingbirds, but of much larger dimensions. Although the birds were the size of crows, they were as exquisite as robins or canaries.

The water and the birds were a delight to experience, but they paled by comparison to the human figure gliding through the water, wearing a crown of flowers in her light brown hair — head held above the small pool with a dignity suggesting complete ownership of her surroundings. As this remarkable female climbed out of the water, Fay couldn't help but envy the attire thus revealed — a dress of such light material that it clung to the body as if part of the air. And as the woman ran her delicately shaped hands down the length of the fabric, drops of water cascaded (all yellow and red, as well as blue) and the spaces she touched dried quickly, leaving a pattern of stylized flowers on the cloth as if drawings had just appeared.

"Who is that?" asked Fay of her feline companion.

"Haven't a clue," answered Kitnip. "But Mrs. Norse told me to trust my instincts. I feel safe here."

"Yes, I agree. No one who looks like that could be an enemy."

"Don't trust appearances alone," answered the cat gravely. "After all, you thought the Tabrik was bad. On the other paw, just because this young female human looks all right doesn't mean she isn't all right!"

"How do we find out?"

Kitnip pleased Fay with the answer: "Since I'm the one with the instincts, I'll go first. Mrs. Norse would want me to."

No amount of surprises in this strange land could compare to the unpleasant discoveries Fay kept making about herself. She loved the cat, but she didn't want anyone leaving little scars of jealousy on her soul. She was beginning to resent Mrs. Norse, even if this amazing personage represented her only hope, because Kitnip prized the good opinion of a stranger over Fay.

This frustration didn't prevent Fay feeling admiration for Kitnip as the plucky little beast crept on little cat's feet over to the strange young woman who at that moment had begun to sing. The voice thus revealed had the quality of tinkling bells. Fay caught herself feeling increased resentment, not for Mrs. Norse this time, but for the strange girl.

Fay had reached that difficult stage of life when nothing ever feels right. This strange young woman seemed perfect in every way, a perfect face with perfect white teeth, a perfect body with every line in all the right places. And she sang in tune.

The trouble was that Fay had become very self-conscious. And not wearing her top didn't help. She had no reason to disparage her own appearance. Everyone, or close enough, thought she was cute. Fay had a good face with a button nose and high cheekbones. Her hair was a pretty shade of auburn and she wore it long. She thought she was ugly because she had freckles and wore glasses, but she was really pretty. And of course, she wasn't wearing her glasses now. She hadn't seen her reflection since receiving the gift of improved eyesight, but she rightly suspected the freckles would still be there.

A little voice in the back of her head told her she was comparing herself to her mother, who was quite a beauty. Somewhere along the way, Fay had made up her mind that she would never be as attractive as that and had given up. Finally, the voice reminded her of another of her books, one about how envy is a worse emotion than jealousy because the latter merely wants want someone else has, while the former is a destroyer that wants no one to possess or enjoy good things.

While Fay was caught up in thoughts of vanity, Kitnip, who never gave her appearance a moment's thought, grew closer and closer to the objective. The closer the cat drew to this new human, the less danger was felt by the naturally cautious feline. When Kitnip prowled right up to sandaled feet, the cat could not resist the impulse to curl up there and start purring.

Which is exactly when the young woman looked down and said, "I'm Jennifer. Who are you?"

Now this was a surprise. Jennifer expected the cat to talk. "I'm Kitnip," came the answer, mixed up with ongoing sounds of purring. "I'm traveling with a young human to the Hive."

"Where is this young human?" asked Jennifer.

"She's waiting for me to tell her it's safe."

"Then tell her."

So Kitnip did. But it's not like Fay hadn't been eavesdropping on every word of the conference. As the girl from Earth stepped into the open, Jennifer exclaimed, "Oh, you're lovely."

Normally a compliment didn't mean much to Fay. But as those golden words left Jennifer's lips, Fay felt a warm glow of satisfaction unlike anything she'd felt before. People were always making her feel like she had to justify herself. Here was someone who accepted her completely on first sight.

"Let's eat!" said Jennifer without further preamble.

"Thank you," said Fay who was indeed hungry by now.

"The food is good," boasted Jennifer, "and best of all, eating it won't make you a slave." Fay and Kitnip exchanged curious glances at that last remark, but it was good to know that their next meal would come with such a high recommendation.

Then Jennifer passed her new companions some flowers! As the hostess was already putting one past the rosy portal of her own lips, Fay screwed up her courage and ate one, too. It tasted awfully good despite appearances and smelling of perfume. She'd swear she was eating cheese. Kitnip, more hesitant, sniffed at the petals of her offering quite a long time before taking a tentative lick at it, then happily gulped down what tasted very much like liver.

Next, wooden cups were produced by Jennifer. These she filled with water from the pool and passed one to Fay while placing the other before the cat. That's when Jennifer noticed the bundle tied up in Fay's blouse. The earth girl wearing nothing on top had not drawn the young woman's attention at all.

"That's a pretty bag," she said.

"It's actually my blouse, a shirt I should be wearing," said Fay, a little embarrassed.

Jennifer blinked her large eyes and smiled prettily at Fay. "Then why are you using it as a container?"

"Because I had nothing else."

"Oh. Please let me give you a sack and you can have your clothing back."

Kitnip rubbed up against Jennifer's leg. She didn't usually take to strangers this quickly, but Fay felt the same way. Jennifer started rummaging around several boulders over by the spring and, *hesto-presto,* came up with an emerald green sack that was so pretty that it took the breath away.

"I can't thank you enough!" said Fay.

"I'll allow you to try," said Jennifer sweetly. "I'll even share my nickname with you. It's Bright Well, for the waters of light. By the way, what are you carrying exactly?"

Exchanging glances with Kitnip, Fay decided to keep no secrets from this person. "Only a few pine cones," she admitted.

"Mmmmmm hhhhmmmmm," was Jennifer's response through closed lips. "Just as I expected. They're only dangerous in the hands of types like you and me, in case you didn't know."

"Sometimes I'm glad I don't have the responsibility of hands," said Kitnip.

"I haven't used them yet," said Fay. "I doubt they'll amount to much."

"Take care," warned Jennifer, reaching out to touch one of the cones as Fay untied her shirt. "They only work against the proper foes, but then they are lethal. That's why Malak works so hard to ban their use from the Seasons."

"What foes?" asked Fay, afraid that she already knew.

Jennifer shrugged and told her: "Monsters, of course."

Chapter Nine
And Through The Woods

When Grandfather, that is to say Malak, that is to say the Dour One, had removed his head from his body and thrown it at Clive (who used to be his nephew), the unfortunate lad nearly fainted. At least the head missed him. All that was left was a puff of smoke where the enemy had stood...and some broken pieces of clay that were his head only a moment before. His minions were nowhere to be seen but they hadn't left puffs of smoke behind to mark their passing.

"How corny can you get?" growled Wolf. "I hate people like that."

"Like what?" asked Clive, who was shaking so badly he had somehow missed the "corniness" of the attack.

"He's the worst kind of show-off," continued Wolf, "just because he has a few tricks — not that many, but enough to intimidate other people! Maybe we're not facing real danger; maybe Mrs. Norse exaggerated the threat. She could have left Kitnip and me out of it."

At that precise moment there was a sound of thunder back beyond the trees. Only how was thunder produced by that very unnatural sky? Clive did not want to contemplate the emptiness above. His sense of direction had always been lousy. Despite this handicap, he was sure the sound had issued from the vicinity of Mrs. Norse's house.

Wolf became as serious as if he'd just been informed that he was going on a vegetarian diet. His ears flattened and his tail went between his legs in the fashion of a dog that's been reprimanded by a stern master. Which, perhaps, he had been.

Clive thought this a good opportunity for expressing his fears. "I don't understand any of this, but I'm glad you're here with me, boy." Wolf wasn't really listening but Clive kept at it with dogged persistence. "I mean, I was scared of Granddad when he was alive, but now he's so much worse. He's not exactly a ghost, is he? Somehow I don't think anything here is a ghost." He shuddered at memory of the dreadful homunculi.

Wolf had recovered sufficiently to pay attention again. ""Boy," the dog began, but the sarcasm was lost on Clive, "I wouldn't know a ghost if it came up and bit me. What's sure is that everything here seems real enough to sink my fangs into. But if this is the worst the bad guys can throw at us...." He caught himself before this line of argument led him back into the treacherous waters of criticizing Mrs. Norse.

"Well, Clive," he changed the subject, "I'm sure it will turn out all right. We'll defeat this unpleasant guy you and I used to know as someone else."

Clive wanted to believe that as wicked as Grandfather had been, the man was human...and now this was an entirely different individual threatening the Gurney family. But Clive knew better. He couldn't forget Pine Lake. Here they faced the essence of the man, completely fulfilled.

Questions itched at the back of Clive's head as if a squadron of fleas had taken up residence there. What sort of world was this before Grandfather came? How long had Mrs. Norse been here? Questions without answers are like cats without mice — they'll keep chasing the little critters until they catch one. Clive had always been more impatient than his sister.

"Wolf," he said, "who are these strange people? Where are we, really?"

The dog's impatience was fully the equal of his one-time owner: "I've already told you everything I can."

"That's not good enough."

"Mrs. Norse will...."

"I don't want to hear that name all the time!!" Clive was so upset that he was shouting. In contrast to how Wolf reacted to the thunder, the dog was unfazed by Clive's outburst. Becoming more expert in gauging his ineffectiveness with others, Clive altered the approach and asked, "How much longer before we reach her house?"

"That depends on the obstacles we face," came the calm reply.

"Exactly!" Clive raised a finger to emphasize his point, which looked somewhat ridiculous when talking to a dog. "We may never get there."

"We sure won't if we stand around here arguing about it."

A sage once observed that you should never try to outstubborn a cat. This was a sentiment with which Clive had to agree. But dogs are more reasonable (according to television commercials at least). At any rate, Wolf was more reasonable, and he was thinking: never try to outstubborn a *teenager.*

"There's something you're not telling me," Clive insisted.

"True," Wolf admitted, softly padding over to where the remains of Malak's "head" lay scattered about the ground like so many dry crusts of bread. "I've told you what I understand. If you're wise, you'll wait for Mrs. Norse to answer questions."

Clive's expression was so pained that Wolf decided to compromise. "OK, I know a few things. That wasn't really your grandfather who was here. It was one of his creatures, formed of the same substance as those little humans...."

"Monsters," Clive corrected his canine friend, "goblins!"

"OK, goblins. This is the same stuff he used to replace your mother and father. Hey, there may even be a replacement of myself by now."

"There may be one of Kitnip, too," added Clive in a low whisper.

"As if anyone would notice," muttered the dog, giving in to the sort of prejudice that humans are above (except when they are not). "That stuff your holding. Take a sniff of it, Clive."

Clive did and instantly wrinkled up his nose. "Ugh," was his honest evaluation.

"What does that smell like to you?"

The Gurneys kept a compost heap in the back yard from a failed effort to start a garden and grow their own vegetables. The tomatoes had worked out, and some flowers, but another dream of self-sufficiency went seriously awry — although not before Clive had been introduced to a most remarkable aroma. This gray stuff in his hand had something of the same quality, but only when it was held up close. The accent seemed to be on rotten eggs mixed with cabbage.

Wolf continued his explanation: "When that fungus type material is eaten on Earth, it's like consuming a kind of poison, and the result immobilizes the victim. Here it has other powers. Malak and Mrs. Norse can use it to make living creatures! They're not the only ones who can do this, but they're the best."

"Poison," said Clive, dropping the piece he'd been holding.

"Maybe that's the wrong word since it doesn't actually kill, not even back home. Mrs. Norse says it doesn't do any harm to eat in this world, not that such pleasant news makes it smell or taste any better. I guess once it's in your intestinal track you're safe from Malak or Norse doing anything tricky with it. Say, I just had a strange thought."

"Just one?" laughed Clive. "You mean everything else you've been saying isn't?"

"No, kid, what I mean is: have you had to go to the bathroom since you've been here?"

Clive thought for a moment. "No, but I haven't eaten recently and I've been too excited to notice...."

"Yeah, well don't sweat it. I was just gnawing the bone with idle speculation."

"Huh?"

"Never mind. The important thing is Mrs. Norse told me if a human eats that stuff, he'll be shown things."

Clive wondered if he shouldn't leave well enough alone instead of pestering Wolf for more information. "Eat poison?" he asked incredulously.

"You're not listening," Wolf admonished him. "The stuff's not poison *here*. It might even answer some of your million questions for all I know."

"Are you saying I should eat it?"

"If you wait, I'm sure that Mrs. Norse will answer your questions, Clive. If you don't want to wait, that's fine with me, so eat it already! But stop asking me questions I can't answer."

Clive pondered the grey fragments at his feet. The truth was that he didn't like making decisions. Reaching down, he picked up another piece of the ugly stuff — a smaller piece this time — and held it gingerly at eye level, turning it around as if he were examining a rare jewel. No, it didn't look very appetizing.

He felt Wolf's eyes on him. The dog had been forthright about his motives. Wolf didn't want to be pestered one moment longer. So Clive should, in good conscience, stop asking the poor pooch questions about THE NATURE OF THINGS ... or open his mouth and chew. A little voice was saying: *Just say no to magic ...* but in a world that seemed to operate on magical principles, such advice was inane.

"Look," said Wolf, "if you want to try it, don't worry. Mrs. Norse says it's safe. I'll stand guard if you do."

"Why would you stand guard?" asked Clive, confused.

"Hey, the food won't kill you but don't forget where we are. This isn't exactly our back yard." They looked at each other, Wolf impatiently and Clive bemused. "Well," said the dog, "what's your decision?"

"OK, OK, I'll eat it...."

"I never said..." began the dog.

"No, I'm sorry," Clive corrected himself. "I meant I'll make a decision. And my decision is IT'S CHOW TIME!"

If it weren't for the permanent grin with which all dogs are cursed, Wolf would have smiled. "So I'll stand guard," he said, taking up his position.

One deep breath later, Clive took a small bite of the dried, fungous substance. The bad news was that it tasted perfectly terrible. The good news was that it didn't require more than one bite to have the desired effect. Clive, first-nighter!

The program wasn't exactly a premiere. He was seeing the same vision that so upset his younger sister when she had her last nightmare: Mom and Dad in transparent boxes, suspended over the yellow fog with snake-like objects floating all around them.

Then suddenly the boxes disappeared, and Mom and Dad fell straight into the fog. Clive wanted to scream but he didn't seem to have a throat or larynx any longer, or a body for that matter. He was only a presence, watching, watching ... but unable to do anything.

He willed himself to follow his parents but couldn't get beneath the thick, yellow fog. As they had fallen, they'd seemed to be moving further apart. He wanted to follow one.

His father was singled out for the honor of continued surveillance. The Clive presence was sinking beneath the mists, falling; and before he knew it, he could see his father far below. The man was naked from the waist up, with a reddish sunburn — and this made sense, because there was a sun in the sky again.

Dad was swinging a scythe. Clive knew it was a scythe because he'd seen one in a comic book about the Grim Reaper. Dad was swinging the wicked looking blade in a wide arc, and cutting down what appeared to be tall stalks of wheat.

As the picture became more clear, Clive was surprised to see that the wheat had faces. He could also hear his father muttering under his breath, "Have to prove myself ... have to be worthy of her ... can't stand her coldness any longer ... maybe I can warm her up with other people's blood ... a sure way to success ... she must take me back, I want her back, I want my wife.... What's mine is mine, mine, mine!"

Then Clive was rising again into the yellow clouds, moving

through mist until it was time to descend again. He swooped down faster this time, to see his mother standing all alone on a barren plain. She was moving some large, flat rectangular objects. The perspective made her appear ungainly although she had always been graceful. The objects were almost transparent and several feet higher than herself. They had semi-transparent supports extending to the ground. Although Clive could see through them, he could tell where the edges were, like drawings in a coloring book before you color them in. The nearest Clive had come to seeing anything like them were stage flats on which he helped paint scenery for the school play.

When Clive was close, he saw that Mom was not as alone as she had appeared. She was surrounded by little creatures jumping up and down. They were humanoid. They were male. They looked a lot like Dad.

As each one would bound up near her face, chattering and smiling, she would move one of the large flats so that it stood between them. No sooner had she done this than another would try to attract her attention and she would repeat her actions with another of the flats. The little creatures varied their approach. Some would shout, some would sing, some would only smile and some would frown. Some performed acrobatic stunts. But no matter what they did, she'd move the tall, thin walls so that they stood between her and their ministrations.

She never uttered a word.

Then Clive was rising again, back into the clouds, hurtling along to the next stop. Nor did he have long to wait. This time he descended to a giant doll house. Somehow he knew it was a doll house, although its proportions were the same as a real one. Fay seemed to be waiting for someone on the porch. She was surrounded by a herd of plastic ponies, big enough to climb on because they were as oversized as everything else.

The Clive presence was surprised that Fay wasn't dressed in doll clothes. She was wearing her two piece bathing suit (the one she'd had to fight with Mom to let her buy with her own hard earned allowance money). She was observing her surroundings with an expression of faint disgust. She went inside and Clive's presence followed. On a pink table in the center of the "living room" were two large bottles with labels attached. One was marked **FACTS** and the other **OPINIONS**.

Sitting down, she proceeded to uncork the bottles, and started pouring the contents of the first one into the second — then she poured the second back into the first. Clive noted a marked similarity to the episode of Mr. Wizard. Fay repeated this seemingly pointless procedure over and over, and as she did so her voice poured out as well: "It's all my fault" — "You shouldn't blame yourself" — "They don't love me" — "I hate them, I hate them" — "Grandfather's a troll and if I only had the money I'd give it to Mom and Dad ... and that would show him!"

Clive was more interested in what his sister was saying than he'd been in the scenes of Mom and Dad. He didn't like it when the force controlling what he saw and heard pulled him out of the giant doll house against his wishes. He willed himself to remain just where he was but to no avail. This had him wondering if the decision to follow his father had truly been his own. But where could he be going now? He'd seen Dad, then Mom, then Fay. There was no one left except....

He didn't like the logical implication. He didn't want to see some weird badness happening to himself. Whatever was next, his feeble will power was no longer part of the equation. He'd been returned to the clouds, moving through the thick mist, and then he was falling again, plummeting to the very scene he most dreaded.

Wondering if he could close his eyes this time led nowhere but to the reminder that he didn't have eyelids. He was a disembodied mind bouncing around space as if trapped in some ultimate Nintendo game. He could no more stop what was happening than a shout can stop a thought.

He saw himself. He was locked in a box on the end of a rope. He could see his own face because there was a small glass panel breaking the smooth expanse of wood near the top of — now he recognized the shape! — the coffin. The rope was tied to a gnarled tree whose naked branches seemed to form a finger pointing to the dark abyss over which the coffin swung. The creaking of the rope was the only sound penetrating another of Clive's senses that somehow functioned without organs. Whatever was happening to him in this trance, he couldn't smell anything.

Back and forth, back and forth … this was more terrible than the other sights. Dad had the freedom to swing his scythe; Mom the freedom of moving her walls; Fay the freedom of a house, and to pour bottles one into the other. In contrast, the Clive of the vision had no freedom of any kind. He was completely dependent on external factors.

The creaking rope made him think of the summer he'd gone sailing with his Uncle Ashley. There had been something reassuring about the repetitive caress of rope on wood. Maybe if he could think about that, he'd banish this experience. But such was the nature of the controlled hallucination that it left no room for any memory, or a desire to create a picture contrary to the present selection.

"No!" He had no voice but somehow he would make his thought heard. "No!" He couldn't conjure up a different picture but he could remember the timbre of his own voice. "NO!!!" Now he could hear himself, he really could, and it came from outside this terrible dream.

He was waking up. But right before he opened his eyes, he heard a woman's voice, so rich and comforting that it completely overwhelmed all objections. It said: "Only you can overcome your problems, but you'll need help. I offer you what is within my power. By saving your family you will help to save far more."

Clive opened his eyes. Eyelids! Watering eyeballs underneath. It was good to be back. Wolf was licking his face. For a moment,

Clive forgot this was more than his good old dog. This was a new friend.

"No danger to report," said Wolf, "but I'm glad you're coming out of it."

Clive must have collapsed at some point. Now he stood up too quickly and felt a wave of dizziness. "Hold on there," said Wolf. "Give yourself a moment."

That was good advice, all right, as Clive gratefully sat back down. "So tell me, kid, what was it like?"

Clive shook his head, as if trying to clear away the residue of his mental journey. "Like dreaming wide awake," he said. "Fay was having dreams like this for months and months. I'm surprised she didn't go crazy."

"How do you know she didn't?" asked Wolf, trying to put humor in his voice, but a talking dog has certain limitations. The awful expression on Clive's face indicated a misfired joke. The dog recovered with: "I mean she likes Kitnip best, doesn't she?"

At last Clive relaxed enough to laugh. He scratched behind Wolf's ears. The dog part could still be reached in more ways than one.

"Hey, you know I'm just kidding about my token cat buddy. So ... were your questions answered?" asked Wolf.

Clive shook his head. "I should have known better. There's more questions than ever! I'll be waiting for Mrs. Norse no matter what!"

"And she's waiting on us. I figure if Malak could have stopped us back there, he would have. Let's press on and get to the house. Besides, I'm hungry."

"Don't you want a moment to forage for food?" asked Clive.

"You must be crazy! I don't want to eat this nature stuff. It's even hard to find back home, and Mrs. Norse promised treats." So saying, Wolf was off and running before he remembered Clive would be even slower now, until the after effects had worn off from his experience.

Stifling a growl, Wolf returned and said, "Rrrrrrrest up, Clive."

While Clive sat cross legged on the ground, feeling stupid, Wolf sniffed around, obviously searching for something. Clive was about to ask if Wolf still had a taste for dried up dung when he thought better of it. Suddenly good manners became a real concern.

He worried that he'd be holding Wolf back because his impatience had led him to eat that damned stuff. He felt like his blood had turned to water, and his heart was beating too fast. Then again, the dog told him it wouldn't hurt him to eat it.

"I'm thirsty," Clive announced without preamble.

"Probably that little meal of yours is to blame, but I'm thirsty, too. And we should have at least this problem solved as soon as I ... hooray, I found it!" Wolf started digging under a thick carpet of leaves. Clive watched as twigs and clots of dirt went flying. When Wolf had made a good sized hole, his front quarters disappeared for a moment, and there was heavy breathing from below. When he had reappeared, he had a big, white bone in his mouth.

"This will fix you right up," announced the dog.

"You've got to be kidding," said Clive, but Wolf dropped the object in his lap.

"Just unscrew the top," said Wolf. Upon closer examination, the bone was actually plastic, and the top did indeed come off. There was water inside. No sooner did he start to drink than he felt much better.

"There are canteens like that buried throughout Autumn," said Wolf.

Clive lifted his face from the spout and, refreshed, lost any hope for diplomacy that deprivation placed in his heart. "I'm beginning to think there's a lot more you know than you've passed on," he said, "but don't suggest I eat anything else!"

Wolf was too tired from digging to argue, but not too tired to resume the journey. Having ascertained that Clive was ready,

the dog set a slow pace. Clive felt so good that he outran Wolf for
thirty whole seconds.

Chapter Ten
The Klave

Jennifer sang to Fay and Kitnip as they ate the sweet food that came in the shape of brightly colored flowers. The flowers were almost too sweet. But they made Fay feel stronger. The cat was eating a smaller flower than Fay's, a dark red bloom. It was pretty easy to guess that this one must taste like meat.

"So, tell me about yourselves," Jennifer suggested.

Fay remembered the title of a book she had been intending to read: *Stranger in a Strange Land.* She'd heard those words in church, too. So she used them to describe herself to Jennifer.

"Well, you are strangers," the lovely girl replied, "but there's nothing strange about this land — at least not until the new monster came."

Kitnip's ears went up at those words, and Fay could guess what would come next. "Do you mean Grand ... I mean, the one Mrs. Norse calls Malak?"

"Oh, do you know *her?*" asked Jennifer bounding up. "Isn't she the most wonderful person? She taught me a dance." Fay had a cousin who was interested in Renaissance dance, and as Jennifer began to sway back and forth, and then take little hopping steps in a formalized style, it reminded the young stranger that no matter how far you travel from home, there will always be reminders of what you've left behind.

But at the moment, Fay was not enjoying the demonstration. She was exasperated at how difficult it was to keep this pretty young thing on any subject for long. The best to be done was to keep trying.

"You were talking about a monster?" Fay tried again.

"Yes," came the languid voice. "The new one."

"Might that be Malak?" the cat volunteered.

"They're all Malak, you know," sighed Jennifer, in the most

matter-of-fact tone. She was starting to sound bored but Fay wasn't about to let their hostess get off that easy.

"Please tell us what you know," requested Fay in a stern voice.

"What could I tell you that you wouldn't find out from Mrs. Norse?"

Oh, the girl was irritating. "Since we haven't seen her yet, how the hell should we know?" Fay was surprised to hear such language coming out of her own mouth. Kitnip's tail went straight up.

The outburst did accomplish something. Jennifer stopped dancing. "I'm sorry," she said, her eyes fluttering. "I didn't mean to make you sad." She sort of glided over and touched Fay's cheek with a most delicate hand. "I'll help you," she said, then kissed Fay on the forehead. "I'd kiss you on the top of your head except you're almost as tall as I am. You must be very tall for your age."

Fay blushed. "Yes, my brother teases me about it."

Jennifer took Fay by the hand and led her over to sit on a flat stone next to the waterfall. "Now I'll tell you about the monster," she said. "Once upon a time...."

"I don't believe this," said the cat in a low sibilant hiss of skepticism.

"... there was a very bad wizard who hated the seasons. He wanted everything to stay the same all the time so he wouldn't need to change his wardrobe or alter his plans because of the weather. But of all the worlds in space and time in which he might take up residence, he was in the very worst place for a person who felt the way he did. You see, he was living right in the center of the Seasons, in a palace where all four Seasons met at the exact point of his throne."

The manner in which Jennifer regarded Fay inspired a nod from her young protegé. Fay leaned forward, eager to hear more.

Jennifer continued: "The evil wizard had a name no one can remember any longer, but he took a new name, Malak, and with the passing of time his new name became a title. He made so much trouble for everyone that the people of the land had to turn to The Original for help."

Jennifer paused as if expecting her young friend to ask the obvious question, but Fay smiled sweetly, assuming: *Wait long enough, and everything has a reason.*

Jennifer laced her fingers together whenever she mentioned the Original, which she began doing with greater frequency: "The Original, of course, created the Seasons, and gave them this home from which to guide secondary worlds. No one would have dreamed that a native of these lands would ever challenge the Seasons! There was a war in which the palace was destroyed. You have seen the remains."

Try as she might, Fay could not remember passing through any monumental ruins recently. She shook her head. Jennifer smiled and said, "You stood on what was once the most magnificent palace in all the universes."

Recognition dawned as Fay gasped, "The stone mountain!"

"The sodden mound o'er which blossomed the hopes of all," intoned Jennifer, without missing a beat. "So it was the Original took on many forms instead of One. You are well aware of the most respected form."

Fay required no extra prompting. "Mrs. Norse," she said, then added, "of course." *Aaaargh, that rhymes,* she thought.

"We love her best because she's closest to the Original. The rest kept breaking up into smaller and smaller parts, until you get me, for instance!" Choosing that moment to curtsy, Jennifer allowed herself the pleasure of enjoying Fay's exaggerated expression.

Unsure whether or not she should bow or kneel before the beautiful woman, Fay asked, "What happened to the people who lived there?"

"They're still around, but in greatly reduced forms. Some are nice and some are nasty — so what would you expect? What's important," said Jennifer, throwing her hair over her shoulder for emphasis, "is that we pieces of the Original have our hands full putting up with all the different people who take turns at being Malak! Mrs. Norse has her hands full. From the beginning, she told the first Malak, as she has told all his successors, how silly it was to oppose the Four Seasons on the grounds that he wanted things always to be the same. The Seasons make up one thing, after all, just in four parts. They're always the same, even if they do provide a little variety. And what's wrong with a little variety, anyway?"

Fay agreed that there was nothing wrong with variety and that she, in fact, had a marked preference for it. Jennifer pressed on: "If you've seen one Malak, you've seen them all! They insist that One Season will have to conquer the other Three for all times and places. Mrs. Norse was surprised that Malak didn't seem to care which Season would prevail over the rest. I suppose it was random chance that he chose Autumn for his first attempt. Mrs. Norse did such a good job of defending that country from him that she made it her permanent home. And incidentally, Malak was destroyed for a while. He tried to divide himself into many pieces just the way the Original did."

"What happened?" Fay blurted out.

"He broke himself! But a force of will was left behind his shattered body, a fiend that wouldn't rest until One won! Oh my, that rhymes." The cat sniffed the air, whiskers twitching the way they always did when there was too much cuteness in the air.

"Why is Mrs. Norse called Mrs. Norse?" asked the cat.

"Because it's her name, silly!" was Jennifer's perfectly reasonable reply. "Ever since the great battle, 'Malak' has been an unhonorary office. Or should that be dishonorary?"

"Dishonorary," opined Fay because she thought it sounded better.

"Non-honorary," Kitnip corrected everyone in sight. "There's something I'd like to know. Wolf and I were grabbed by humanoid things Malak had sent to replace Mr. and Mrs. Gurney..."

"Slaks," said Jennifer in a cold voice. "We call them Slaks."

"Yessss," purred the cat, "a good name for them. I thought I was about to use up all my remaining lives, if I may draw upon a venerable human superstition. But Mrs. Norse rescued us, gave Wolf and me a briefing at her house, and then before we had our bearings, wrinkled her nose or whatever she does, and I was with Fay and I assume Wolf is with Clive. A real shame, too, because I was just becoming acquainted with a really handsome Tabby...."

"Kitnip!" Fay was genuinely put out.

"Sorry," said the cat, "but I want to know what we're up against. Is it possible to oppose Malak? If not, is there anywhere where we can hide from him?"

Jennifer suggested they go for a walk, as much to help digest their food as absorb the feast of information following those innocent sounding words, Once upon a time. Jennifer took Fay by the hand and led her young friend to the opposite side of the alcove, while Kitnip's dark shape darted in and about their smooth, white legs.

"Now, as to Kitnip's question," Jennifer pontificated, but delightfully, "the problem was that the forces released by Malak couldn't be reversed. They had become part of reality, the same as the Seasons. They were like a kind of bad weather." Fay wanted to ask what they used for weather around here but the breath Jenifer took was insufficient to get a word in edgewise.

At least Jennifer maintained a chatty tone: "When the first Malak tried to split himself into little Malaks, doing something only the Original can really do, he still accomplished a bad thing. Bits and pieces of himself spread throughout the Universes and infected people. These little bits would drift in the air of a particular world until they were inhaled by all sorts of people and animals; but only a certain kind of person was in danger of becoming infected."

"I see where this is going," said Kitnip.

"Boy, did they come to the right place when they found Grandfather."

"You wouldn't be here," Jennifer told them, "unless your world provided the new monster. There should also be signs and portents in your own sphere."

"I understand," said Fay. "Global warming?"

"Coming right after the new ice age!" sniffed the cat, unimpressed.

"Huh?" asked Jennifer and Fay as one.

While Fay was trying to figure out how Kitnip knew so much, Jennifer said, "You're out of my depth, but soon you'll meet someone who can handle almost anything."

They hadn't walked that far from the site of their pleasant picnic, but they had been in a secluded place, closed in without much of a view. Fay had no idea how near they had been to their destination until they walked over a hill, crowned with tall trees.

They had been only a few hundred yards from a most amazing sight. Instinctively, Fay's hand went for the makeshift sack of pine cones at her side. She could feel Kitnip rubbing up against her as if to say everything was all right.

The gigantic glass hive loomed on the horizon. Maybe a thousand of the semi-transparent men could be seen working inside and outside the edifice. From the stone mountain, it had been impossible to see inside.

Once again, Fay was dumbfounded by a world without shadows. The effect was as if everyone floated above the ground instead of actually touching. If she ever got home again, she'd never take shadows for granted. Even the most solid looking objects were given a quality of insubstantiality by the absence of shadows. In the case of the skeleton men, who didn't appear real to begin with, the sight was truly disorienting.

Another oddity was that with all the feverish activity, one would expect noise. There was only a slight rustling and murmuring to be heard. If you weren't experiencing it for yourself you would assume these were forest sounds, the gurgling of a brook and perhaps the foraging of squirrels. As they drew near, other sounds could gradually be made out — a low humming and a persistent sighing.

The figures inside the glass building were working on some kind of machines that were made from all sorts of things: wood, metal, stone, glass … everything except the strange, grey substance Jennifer had warned Fay not to eat.

Fay was fascinated by what the people were doing on the outside. They seemed as naked as the others except for large belts of some dark material that held tools. (She had gotten past the point of thinking of them as creatures. Whatever they were, they were most certainly people; but she didn't like the name, Tabriks.)

They were tending to animals that were swimming in circular ponds surrounding the great hive. These were turtle-like creatures with almost perfectly triangular shells. They flourished in pairs, one large and one small, attached by a rubbery tube that went from the exact center of one shell to the other. This meant that the big one tended to drag the little one around.

Several of the skeleton folk were poking at the turtles with long poles. The idea seemed to be to remind the large turtles they had the smaller turtles connected to them. A powdery food being sprinkled across the surface of the water was easily consumed by the big ones, leaving nothing for their smaller partners if they weren't prodded to remember.

One of the Tabriks was going from pool to pool, peering at the denizens of the water through over-sized spectacles. When the figure doing the inspecting was satisfied, he would simply nod at one or two of the turtle couples, and one of the workers would use his pole (they had grappling devices on the end) to fish some of the turtles out.

Next, the two turtles would be carried over to a large object that seemed to be growing out of the ground. The top portion seemed to be a collection of small caves thrown together pell-mell, while the bottom part resembled the trunk of a gigantic tree. When the skeleton man positioned the two small creatures, still dripping wet, over one of the caves, hanging helplessly, he pulled out a pair of scissors from a belt that was his only attire. He snipped the cord! The two turtles separated and fell, side by side, into the waiting dark holes.

"Isn't it beautiful?" asked Jennifer.

"If you say so," Fay replied uncertainly.

"They're mating!" reported Kitnip. "That can't be anything else." There were slippery sounds emanating from the holes, and occasionally the flash of something glistening down there in the dark.

"It's the Klave," intoned Jennifer.

"Whatever they're doing," said Fay, surprising herself by the depths of peevishness she detected in her own voice, "how is this going to help my family? I don't have anyone...." (and even as the words escaped from her lips, she knew she was doing Kitnip an injustice) ... but she couldn't stop the torrent: "I'm tired and I'm afraid."

"If you were really afraid," came a kindly voice, "you wouldn't carry on like that."

Turning slowly, she saw one of the Tabriks, her terrible skeleton men, standing right behind her. Only this time she felt just fine about him.

The forest of Autumn was cool without being clammy or wet. With no mornings or nights, it was a mystery when, if ever, dew clung to the brightly colored leaves. But however it was accomplished, the fresh smell was refreshing.

Clive and Wolf felt strong and weren't even a little bit tired. This was good, because the woods were wide and deep. Since drinking the water Wolf found, Clive was reinvigorated. He was still hungry but able to ignore the empty ache at the center of his stomach. As he ran, he felt like he was floating above the ground.

"It's here!" cried Wolf, loping forward. He'd found a path, no small feat with all the leaves around. Clive was filled with joy. After all, paths generally lead somewhere. Their destination must be near ... especially with the remarkable totem pole towering up ahead, and growing larger with every step.

Wolf was so happy that he was running up and down a rock studded incline next to the path. He even let himself bark. There must not be any dangers here. Clive relaxed.

They ran the rest of the way.

As Clive took his first step out of the woods, birds began to sing. They seemed to be mostly above and behind him, but he didn't waste any time trying to see them. His attention was riveted by the house he'd spied through the telescope on the mountain of stone, only it was far more dramatic experienced close at hand.

The house was more than secluded. Viewed from any angle, it was well hidden unless you came up right on top of it. And yet as he moved closer, Clive noticed how peculiar it was that the place had a neatly kept lawn. Even if raked every day, a cascade of leaves and twigs would surely cover it within a few hours.

The scene was as perfect as something out of a display window at a department store, awash in the glow of good credit. The house was of wood and brick, with just a dab of paint here and there to show off its best features. There were two stories with the largest lightning rod this side of a Frankenstein movie jutting from the roof and pointed at the totem pole. The perfectly maintained lawn enclosed the house like a green doughnut.

The path Wolf had been following came to an abrupt end at the edge of the grass. Wolf turned to Clive as if the human member of the team should do something. All Clive knew was that he didn't like upstairs windows. These seemed to be gazing upon him with sad, dusty eyes.

"Too weird," was how he appraised the tall, wooden mailbox rising incongruously out of the leaf blanketed ground directly in front of the untouched lawn. On the front of the box was a great cat's head with emerald eyes shining.

"Wonder how she gets mail out here," said Wolf. The dog sniffed at the edge of the green sea. This was the most remarkable proof yet to Clive that they were in a topsy-turvy world: a dog hesitating to go on the grass! Clive decided to take the initiative. There was no other way to reach the door. Besides, Wolf told him to go first.

Even through his shoes, it was as if he could feel the softness of each individual blade. It was like walking on foam rubber. He marched forward to the front door.

There was no doorbell, no heavy knocker, no way of making noise but to bring his fist down on the old wood. He did just that, knocking once, twice, three times. Meanwhile, Wolf had crept up behind him. Their roles had changed subtly. The dog was not sure of himself here.

From inside they heard a rustling, and then the mewing of a cat. The door opened on well-oiled hinges without the slightest squeak. With exacting little ballet steps, a cat emerged. Clive could feel how uncomfortable Wolf was as the feline walked around them, scrutinizing every detail, before disappearing inside.

All this time, the door was only half open. Now it opened all the way. A voice from deep inside called out: "Welcome."

Chapter Eleven
Mrs. Norse

They entered the dark interior of the old house. Of course, if this were the only house in the whole world, there wasn't anything that could be used for comparison. But it sure felt old, smelling of mothballs and clean rosewood, of delicate incense and furniture polish.

In the hallway, there was a noisy grandfather clock keeping time with heavy monotony. Clive felt that he should tiptoe past the antique as if he didn't want to disturb the repetitive ticks and tocks with his own sounds. It was that kind of place.

He'd never been in a house like this before. The closest he'd come was at a museum, in the Early American section. More than a carefully preserved house, this was like stepping inside a glass case where a history lesson in old wood and older ceramics was laid out under golden lights, with big DO NOT TOUCH signs everywhere. Only there were no signs.

Wolf let Clive take the lead. It was easy to sense how uncomfortable the dog was. The brown and white cat that met them at the door expressed a disdain far beyond anything Kitnip had ever shown.

Clive was nervous, too. At least he was until he stepped into the living room. Mrs. Norse was waiting for them. One look at her put Clive at his ease.

She was standing in the center of the room, surrounded by cats. She had a full head of silver-white hair, but it didn't make her appear old. Her smooth, strong face suggested hearty middle age; the few wrinkles around her eyes and neck seemed less the result of aging as the final touch to a work of art. The hair was combed upwards so that different strands found their own eccentric peaks. A gigantic pair of owl glasses, supported by a sizeable nose, dominated her face. The dress she wore was an old fashioned mother hubbard affair, the primary color of which was lavender.

"Hello," she said in a musical voice that made the single word into both a fond greeting and question.

"Mrs. Norse, I presume," said Clive, regaining enough confidence to try and be funny. For the first time since stepping foot in this world, he felt at ease. Wolf was happy to see her and promptly forgot how uncomfortable he'd been a moment before. His tail wagged so hard you'd never know he was surrounded by cats. After all, it is one thing to grow up with a cat as a friend; is quite another to be deposited in the enemy camp, so to speak. "Woof," was all he could think to say under the circumstances.

"You are both more than welcome," said Mrs. Norse. "I bear the responsibility of bringing you here. Please sit down, Clive."

The nearest place to sit was a comfortable looking chair that had a partly finished cross-stitch lying on the seat cover. As he reached down to move the item lest he damage it, he noticed the subject of the picture taking shape with each little piece of colored thread. It was a family: a mother, a father, a daughter and a son. As he looked more closely at the nearly finished creation, he couldn't help but recognize the all too familiar faces.

"I must be getting careless," said Mrs. Norse, stepping forward to relieve him of the item. "It wouldn't do to have you sitting on my modest handiwork."

She felt his reluctance in letting it go. "Oh, don't worry," she comforted him. "It is a picture of your family, but that's all. Not a smidgen of magic to it!" He did feel relieved when she said that, but wasn't sure why.

As she moved off in the direction of the kitchen, more cats came into the room. A lot more cats. Clive glanced over at Wolf to make sure that he was all right. Apparently, the presence of Mrs. Norse was sufficient to keep everyone well behaved.

"You mustn't think that everything here is more than it appears," she said as she entered the kitchen, her voice rising so that she could still be heard. "Nature has a purpose here, the same as man-made artifacts in your world, but that doesn't make everything you see into a symbol."

He didn't have a clue what she was talking about but appreciated the clattering sound of pots and pans. She must be making something to eat. "Sometimes a cross-stitch is just a cross-stitch," she finished, as she reappeared carrying a wooden tray laden with tea and cookies.

"That's the silliest thing I've ever hoid," said one of the cats in a perfect imitation of Groucho Marx.

"Please put a sock in it, Sigmund," replied another of the cats.

Clive marveled at the fact that he would have been more surprised if the cats didn't speak. While he was at it, he was also amazed that despite a roomful of cats, there wasn't the least odor of catbox, or that aroma that comes from a lot of them being together. There were things about this world he could definitely come to enjoy, if he gave himself a chance. While he pondered such matters, a white kitten began to laboriously climb up his pants leg.

"What flavor tea would you like, young man?" asked Mrs. Norse, leaning down and offering him the tray.

"Do you have a Coke, or something like that?" he asked, embarrassed the moment the words were out of his mouth.

"He'll catch on, give him time," said Wolf in a most annoying tone of voice. Clive kept forgetting his dog, the dog, had already had dealings with the lady of the house.

"There's nothing wrong with your request, but we only have tea here. I'll tell you what. How about we make one of my special teas taste any way you like?"

"Will it be cold?" he asked, wincing as the kitten navigated past his kneecap.

"He's pickier than you are," complained a fat Persian to a crazed looking Siamese.

"As cold as a shard of ice, as frosty as the soul of a giant," Mrs.

Norse replied. This bit of unexpected poetry left Clive with his mouth open, a condition quickly remedied by a tall frosty glass pushed in his direction. He hadn't seen anything on the tray but teacups and cookies a moment ago; but now this pleasure was pressed on him at the same moment the kitten settled itself comfortably in his lap.

He gulped the first swallow. It was so cold that it made his teeth tingle. He got out a thank you, but couldn't leave well enough alone. His usual problem was saying one more thing than necessary. "Are you a witch?" he blurted out.

The lady allowed silence to settle over them. The kitten sensed Clive's tension and departed more swiftly than it had arrived. There was no purring anywhere in the house.

There was a definite school-teacherish quality about Mrs. Norse. She proceeded to prove it: "Always be careful of the manner in which you use words. They have meanings, words do. As to your question, no one has sufficient authority to decide such matters except school librarians ... and witches, of course!"

A black cat laughed. Either that, or it was getting ready to spit up a fur ball.

Wolf decided to help out poor Clive. "I'm sure he meant nothing by it, My Lady." It was the first time Clive had heard Wolf address her formally. She inclined her head in a manner that suggested everything was all right. A little voice in the back of his head was replaying dialogue from a classic movie: *Are you a good witch or a bad witch?* Best to leave well enough alone.

Meanwhile, an even more ungracious chattering was going on in the back of his skull to the effect that Wolf and Mrs. Norse were keeping secrets from him, and just who the hell did they think they were not to level with him? Fortunately he stifled the impulse to articulate any part of that special pleading. "You haven't come all this way, Clive, not to have satisfaction," announced Mrs. Norse.

"Can you tell me what happened to my sister?"

"I'm glad you ask about her first. She is your comrade in this adventure of yours. She is safe."

Clive was greatly relieved. He wondered if he should feel guilty about not having as much concern for his parents, but he really didn't. It was as if they had abandoned Fay and him long before the originals were kidnapped, stolen, replaced....

Mrs. Norse observed the emotions playing over Clive's face but said nothing. He took another swallow of the cold beverage. Then Mrs. Norse asked, "Clive, why do you think you and your sister have so few friends?"

This thoroughly unexpected inquiry fell like a physical blow. It was one thing to be asked such a question by Grandfather, but quite another to be asked by her. Here he was bracing himself for mighty quests, impossible dangers, monsters of every shape and size ... and she goes and hits him with a question like that.

But wait! Why was he thinking of Mrs. Norse in this way? She hadn't caused this mess, as far as he knew. It was Grandfather's fault, or whatever he had become. There was no cause to blame this person who only seemed interested in helping what was left of the Gurney family.

"I'd like a moment to think about it," he said, carefully.

Mrs. Norse's voice was more musical than ever as she said, "Trust to memories, trust in dreams."

Dreams. That was one thing Fay and he had in common now. Were they not sharing the same delusion? What did they call it at school when they had the anti-drug lectures? Hallucinations. Freaking out. His parents talked about having bad trips in their college days.

Yet even as these thoughts were racing through his mind, he was already discounting them. This fantastic world was a real place. In some ways, it seemed more real, more solid, than what he'd left behind. Every passing minute made the land of his birth recede a little further. The nightmare had begun in the old world with Grandfather and his threats. Now it would be resolved, one way or another, right here.

The dreams to which Mrs. Norse referred had to be the ones Fay kept telling him about, and that he received a personal taste of earlier. Those dreams forced him back into contemplating the last thing he wanted to remember. Better to fight with strange forest creatures than have to think about himself!

"Mom and Dad never made it easy for us," he said in a low voice. "They wouldn't let us bring friends home or stay overnight at their houses."

Mrs. Norse seemed to be speaking to him over a great distance when she asked: "Was it always that way?"

Clive was becoming unhappier by the minute. He hadn't thought about these matters very much, but had to admit that all the really bad stuff occurred in the last few years, when the family fortunes took a nosedive. There had been sunny days before that, happy memories, but the storm clouds had rolled in and everything changed.

Dad was mad all the time. Mom cried all the time. At first her tears had been from frustration at their situation, the same as Dad. But then her tears were the way she let her anger out ... and Dad became the *situation* to her. She wanted to go back to college. He criticized her for not caring enough about the children. Clive and Fay came to fear both of them.

He'd almost managed to forget all of this and now Mrs. Norse was forcing him to remember. He looked at her, catching the reflection of his face in her polished glasses. There was no hope of transferring his hatred to her, much as he might like to blame the nearest person at hand. He just couldn't feel that way about her, just as he couldn't really feel too badly about his parents.

There was only one adult, one relative, that all his dark emotions could settle on as a fog of soot settles on towns that can no longer breathe. And that one had earned every ounce of enmity.

"Mrs. Norse, I have to ask you something. Is it wrong to hate?" She seemed the exact sort of person to ask such a question.

"Please forgive my bad manners," she replied. "I forgot to offer you a cookie."

He took a cookie off the tray. It was no ugly grey thing but a big chocolate chip cookie, Clive's favorite kind. But even a flavor as fine as this wouldn't distract him. Mrs. Norse was avoiding the question.

Or was she? In one graceful motion she placed the tray on the coffee table next to the couch, and glided over to the bookcase, the hem of her long dress rustling across the polished floor. The cats surrounded her legs in a sea of fur. The object she was after was not in the case, however. It was a large red book in its own stand, atop an onyx table. As she lifted the book, Clive could see its reflection in the glossy surface of the table, making him think of a lake frozen over in winter — cool thoughts for a mild day in Autumn.

She brought him the book, passing it to him with the special care one would give a baby. The book had a single design threaded in silver at the center of its crimson cover: a circle divided into four portions by a horizontal and a vertical line. Some books have character, made up from the dust of musty libraries, and a texture that only comes when they've been passed down from one generation to the next. Anything rough has been made smooth as a polished stone. This was that kind of book.

He hesitated before opening it. He wanted her to say something. She did: "Clive, never try to talk yourself out of your own experience. Never deny the reality of an emotion. You know what it means to hate. You also know what it means to love. But neither emotion runs very deep in you. The only way that happens is when you've lived long enough to forgive. Then you must choose."

Reaching out with delicate long fingers, she helped him turn the pages. It was a book of pictures. The remarkably intricate designs were of odd shapes he'd never seen in his Geometry textbook. But as he observed the page, something much odder than the drawings caught his attention. The pictures faded, to be replaced by words in a foreign language he no more understood than he did the drawings.

The letters were strange little squiggles and dashes and dots. As he studied them, they started moving and swimming around on the page. He closed his eyes in disbelief, but when he opened them again, the show was still going on.

He seemed to be looking at a page of instructions from a computer manual, like the one he had studied when Dad announced he'd be getting an Apple any day now. (Dad didn't like it when Clive told him that his favorite teacher at school said Apple was the worst system you could buy because there was a worm in it; and the merger with IBM only meant there would be lots of apple sauce.) But the symbols weren't really the same as what he had seen then. They were merely similar.

Before he could make heads or tails of it, the page changed again. This time it appeared to be in columns of Chinese writing; at least what Clive took to be Chinese writing. Next came something very much like Egyptian hieroglyphics, or maybe it really was the language of the Pharaohs. He wouldn't know but just thinking about it seemed to bring up pictures, in faint outline, behind the cryptic messages on the page. Was that a pyramid filling in the left page? Did a sphinx rise from desert sands to hold court on the right page? The style of illustration was very fine, with thin black lines and a definite exaggeration which helped bring the figures to life.

"This is like watching a movie," he said, expressing the highest compliment possible for his generation. "But I don't get it." Out of the corner of his eye, he saw Wolf turning in a circle, the way dogs will, before lying down. The cats made room for him, although most of them were curling up in more comfortable locations. It's as if they all knew this was going to take some time.

"You are reading *The Book of the Seasons*," whispered Mrs. Norse in a reverential tone of voice. "The book is searching to find the best way of communicating with you, but you need to help."

"How?"

"Through what we've been discussing — love and hate. Provide it with a focal point, something personal."

There was no hesitation on Clive's part. He was too worried about his sister for that. He thought about her. He thought hard. And as he did so, the pages changed. On the left was an illustration of Fay visiting with a most peculiar and diversified company. The most striking personage was a man whose skeleton was visible. Judging by Fay's happy, relaxed expression, she had become accustomed to the unusual.

Other figures in the drawing were not as "Halloweenish" as the skeletal gentleman. He was glad of that as he was still coming to grips with the creatures that frightened him so badly in the woods. He especially liked the appearance of a very beautiful woman with flowers in her hair. She reminded him of an older girl at school.

He was glad to see Kitnip in the picture. At least Fay hadn't made the journey alone. He wondered if that cat had been any more informative with Fay than the dog had been with him. While he contemplated the lack of cooperation attendant upon newly liberated pets, words began forming on the page opposite the illustration.

They looked like this:

To return whence you've never been;
to go whither you don't know;
to see the blinding, hear the deafening, taste the tasteless
and smell the emptiness of inner depths;
to touch the fire and live through its embrace;
to do all these things, one must be invited to the Other Side and
arrive at your destination by going the other way.

"Well, that's as clear as mud," said Clive, turning the other page. He was pleased that the next part of the text at least had something to do with the picture on the previous page. There was a new picture now, a picture of himself reading the book!

The new words read:

And so it came to pass that the saviors of the Seasons entered into the Land. If they were to prevail, they would be as the saviors before them, each different and yet each the same in victory. For only if Lord Malak destroyed the balance of all worlds, by making the Four into the One, would the efforts of Lord Clive and Lady Fay be in vain....

Clive did a slow double-take when he read that. Lord Clive? Lady Fay? Was this a joke? One look at Mrs. Norse's smile told him otherwise.

He resumed reading:

Jennifer the One had but recently finished introducing the Lady Fay to the Lord High Mayor of Spring when a new individual entered the scene. "Oh no," said the mayor, "it's Mr. Wynot." Mr. Wynot was a middle-aged man dressed in white shirt and shorts with a white pith helmet on his head, and beaming with a full mouth of teeth just as blindingly bright as the rest of him.

"How about those turtles?" asked Mr. Wynot. "They're really in the soup, huh?"

Chapter Twelve
Chores

"How about those turtles?" asked Mr. Wynot. "They're really in the soup, huh?"

Fay decided that pretty soon nothing would surprise her anymore. At least this new character had a human appearance.

"You are most welcome here, Lord High Mayor of Summer," the Tabrik greeted the newcomer.

"Thank you, Lord High Mayor of Spring," replied Mr. Wynot, bowing low so that his helmet fell off, revealing a full head of snow white hair.

"He always does that," said Jennifer, giggling.

"The spirit of Spring is lovely as always," said Mr. Wynot. Having yet to recover his headgear, he had no problem bowing low again, and pressing his lips to Jennifer's fingers.

Fay had never thought of curtsying before, and thought it would be an embarrassing action to perform. But Jennifer made it appear graceful and attractive. When the well aged hand of the older man took hers, she surprised herself by doing as Jennifer had done. Curtsying wasn't difficult. The interesting part of it was that bending the knees and doing a partial squat could look so good.

"Ah my dear," said Mr. Wynot, his white mustache trembling ever so slightly, "you are warm to the touch. There's a subtle little fire coursing through your skin."

"That must be my sunburn," answered Fay. "Or what's left of it." Fay sorrowfully observed the fading pink on her arm that she had hoped would be turning brown right about now. One thing was certain: she wouldn't be getting a suntan in a world without a sun! And yet Mr. Wynot's skin was pleasantly brown, making a nice contrast against the whiteness of his hair and clothes. It didn't appear to be his natural color, but Fay wasn't about to follow this line of inquiry. Maybe you could get a tan from magic, but even if true, Jennifer's pale white skin suggested not everyone wanted one.

"Ah, methinks it's the fire of youth," said Wynot, inhaling the perfume of her skin. She couldn't help noticing the large veins in his hands, and the wrinkles around his wrists. This was the first example of age she had seen here, although she assumed from the way everyone spoke of her that Mrs. Norse wore the signs of age as well. The difficulty in considering these matters was the absence of any way to measure anything in this crazy place. And Fay had not seen a single child.

As if privy to her young companion's thoughts, Jennifer asked a question of her old acquaintance: "Isn't she a bit young for you?"

Mr. Wynot literally beamed in response! "Those of us who measure our years by the age of the Seasons find every mortal breath as fresh as a daisy, be it newborn or grandmother." Having unburdened himself of his Thought for the Day, he caught the critical expressions of his companions. "But, of course, she is but a child as you say," he added hurriedly, releasing her hand.

With that highly refined obliviousness that is both the charm and burden of youth, Fay insisted, "I'm not a child!"

"Age resents youth," said Kitnip. "This isn't a problem unique to humans."

Fay was glad to have Kitnip on her side despite the cat's being middle aged; she picked up Kitnip before asking permission (when a cat says no, it means no) but Kitnip offered no resistance. She purred instead, and Fay felt a whole lot better.

Meanwhile, Mr. Wynot retrieved his pith helmet, and contrived to make himself the center of attention again. "Yes, it's true about youth and age. But do not forget that youth resents age, too! Many a time I've failed to receive the appreciation due me for many a mighty battle against the forces of evil. Why, just the other day I was asked to recount the tale of...."

"Oh," said the Tabrik leader.

"No," added Jennifer.

The proof of Mr. Wynot's greatness lay in his inability to notice any hints, much less pay attention to them: "Why I fought the original Malak, I did." Fay could tell from just glancing at Jennifer and the Tabrik that there was nothing special about Wynot's claim among this group. He continued: "Malak liked turning his enemies into different sorts of things in those days. He'd figured out that it wasn't very smart to change them into mice or frogs or birds, or frankly any sort of creature that could still get around and cause trouble. He finally settled on the notion of transforming them into rocks. But I was not afraid of him."

The Tabrik leader intervened. "Our young visitor is unversed in the nature of our struggles. You have not told her how our powers are balanced, and that none of the incarnations of Malak has yet succeeded in making any of us truly vulnerable." The semi-transparent head fixed her with watery eyes beyond which yawned the two black holes of the skull's sockets. Where before she dreaded such a sight she was now calm.

The Tabrik continued: "As each season was made to have its own special protectors and avatars, so too was each an environment in which life could grow and develop. Malak has twisted and destroyed much of this life through Time! But he could not do this to every individual who might be under the conscious protection of one of us."

"We couldn't protect everyone all the time," lamented Jennifer.

"Not if we were going to maintain the integrity of the Seasons, which remains our primary task," clarified Mr. Wynot.

Fay didn't have to hear the rest to know what was coming. Only worlds with Winter and Spring and Summer and Autumn were linked to this place, as sort of reflections. All this reminded her of a book she once read right before summer vacation. Clive teased her about studying advanced subject matter when she wasn't required. She could never convince him that she just liked to read!

This particular book had been about ancient Greek thinkers, people who were called philosophers. The father of philosophy was a man named Plato and one of his central ideas was the dumbest thesis Fay had ever encountered — at least it had seemed dumb until today.

Plato told a story about shadows and a cave. Men sat inside the cave, facing a wall on which shadows were cast. They were tied up so that they couldn't look anywhere else. All they ever saw were these shadows. Behind them other men carried a variety of objects past giant burning torches, and by this means shadows were cast. Not unnaturally, the men who only saw the shadows concluded that the shadows must be the reality.

Fay hadn't given this stuff much thought at the time but now the strange picture came back into her head, and it was starting to make some kind of sense. The world she lived in was a shadow if it could be so profoundly affected by what transpired somewhere else. Since coming here, she had only been in this one country of Spring, but it had more of a quality of *springness* about it than anything she had ever experienced on Spring break.

She didn't have to go to Mr. Wynot's Land of Summer to guess how much more *summery* it was than the one she'd left on earth. Likewise, the same had to be true of the other two seasons. She hated to think just how cold Winter was here, the frigid home of Malak ... of Grandfather.

The snapping of fingers brought her out of her reverie. It was Mr. Wynot. He was laughing. "Well, my esteemed fellow mayors, it appears I'm not the only bore in all of space and time. You lost this darling's attention with a Tabrik tale."

"Not at all," said Jennifer, wrapping her arms around Fay's thin shoulders. "She was comprehending truth at a higher level, weren't you dear?"

"What happens here affects my home," she said. Nodding heads made her think of so many Halloween apples in a barrel of water. "Mrs. Norse told Clive and me so in her letter ... before it was ruined. But I don't understand what my parents have to do with it."

"It always begins with personal problems. That's how Malak works," said Mr. Wynot.

"The help they need is in themselves," said the Tabrik.

"And in the Tabriks' most popular export," said Mr. Wynot. "The eggs of the Klave make all the difference. They'll fix up the most damaged relationships. Out with the old and in with the new."

"Stop it!" Fay screamed, pulling lose from Jennifer. "Stop it, stop it, stop it!!! You're talking about my parents! Not some toys ... or children!" She was so upset that the others pulled back from her, genuinely surprised by her sudden wrath.

Fay wanted to stop herself but something in her made her go on, getting more upset all the time. "People are divorced all the time," she cried. "It's not the end of the world, if they're not taken away! Half my friends' parents are divorced. More than half, and they're happy. I mean, they're as happy as anybody is."

Her shouting was heard by some of the Tabriks working nearest to them. One paused for a moment, two of the turtle-like creatures hanging uncertainly from the end of his pole, and starting to bump into each other as they slowly swung back and forth.

Fay was crying. Emotion came off her in a great wave, drenching her newfound friends in a kind of pain that was alien to them. Yet how could they be expected to empathize with someone whose life is so uncertain and happiness so fleeting as a human being? They wore the human form but what did that really mean? Did they get sick? Did they have to struggle for daily existence? It was obvious they had conflict, if not with each other, then with their true enemy. But did their little arguments ever amount to serious bickering, much less an actual break in friendship?

Did they even understand friendship?

These questions raced through Fay's mind as tears trickled down her face. These incredible beings couldn't know what Mom and Dad had been through, or the night terrors of a little girl praying to God that Mommy would stop crying, and Daddy stop shouting; a little girl hoping that she wouldn't hear worse things. Nightmare sounds. End of sanity sounds. The sounds that finally came when Dad went for Clive.

Jennifer reached out and tentatively touched Fay on the shoulder. Fay didn't pull away. Jennifer touched her fingers to adolescent tears. She placed those fingers to her lips and tasted the salt; and tasted something more.

"We're moving too fast," she said to all of them. "Mrs. Norse had no choice but to bring these children here because of the new Malak, and what he did to their parents. That doesn't excuse our being impatient or rude."

"Or too damned mysterious," added the cat, whom Mr. Wynot, for one, had forgotten was there.

Jennifer's mentioning of children in the plural brought Fay back to earth, in a manner of speaking. "Clive!" she blurted out. "Where is he? What's happened to him."

"He's probably with Mrs. Norse by now and safer than we are," said Kitnip.

"Probably isn't good enough," she said through trembling lips, but at least she'd stopped crying. "Is there a way to be sure?"

"Sure," said Mr. Wynot. "You can see Clive any time you want."

"I can?"

"But first you'll have to go swimming," said Jennifer. Kitnip was not at all pleased.

Kitnip was not at all pleased.

Clive stopped reading at that point, transfixed by the illustration of the cat's face in extreme closeup. Kitnip might be talking now, the same as Wolf, but in one respect the cat was still perfectly normal: she hated water.

"You've stopped reading," said Mrs. Norse.

"Fay wants to contact me! What do I do?" Somehow the book seemed inadequate all of a sudden. And as he held it tightly in his hands, and realized it was just a book, after all, he started to get mad.

He quickly learned that the single most annoying aspect about Mrs. Norse was that she knew what you were thinking before you did. Or else she was a very good guesser.

To prove the point, she said, "You think this is a trick, don't you?"

He knew better than that. It was like spending days inside a magic shop and then complaining when someone pulled a rabbit out of a hat.

"Clive, you will be with your sister before long and you will see your mother and father as well. Before you can be of any real use to them, however, you must be tranquil in your own heart."

"How?" he asked. He looked at the book but the pages had become mysterious again, in language he couldn't decipher.

"Are you hungry?"

He'd thought he'd been a short time before. A little bit of food went a long way around here. The cookie he'd eaten was like a full meal. He wasn't thirsty after the one drink either.

"No," he told her, "I'm fine."

"Me, too!" Wolf contributed. The dog would eat almost anything put before him and then yelp for more. Giving him speech was less of a miracle than satisfying his appetite.

"Are you tired?" asked Mrs. Norse of Clive, in the same even tone of voice.

Now that was a different matter. No sooner had she said the words than his eyes felt heavy and his head began to nod forward. She must be some kind of hypnotist at least, all questions of witchcraft aside.

"I hadn't felt tired until you said it ... I was a little tired after I ate that stuff ... and saw Mom and Dad." He hated the way his tongue was becoming heavy and he couldn't keep his eyes open. He was sure he'd been fine until Mrs. Norse took him in charge, but now he was too drowsy to stay awake.

"There is no night here, and you need to take a nap," she told him as from a distance. "Then you'll be ready to perform an important task."

All he could think of was sleep. "I don't want to dream," he said, slurring his words.

"You are living the dream."

The sound of the purring cats grew louder. In fact, they started purring in unison. In and out, in and out, like listening to a motor revving up. As he listened, his eyes grew heavier and he slumped in his chair.

"You just take your nap, and then you can do a little chore around the house," said Mrs. Norse. As if in a dream, she lifted him as though he weighed no more than a few ounces. She carried him into another room where she put him to bed and told him, "No pictures for you now, nothing to interpret or worry over. Your soul is tired."

The next thing he remembered was opening his eyes and lifting his head from the large feather pillow on which it had been resting. He was completely refreshed. He wondered how long he had been asleep but there was no way to tell from the unchanging light outside his window. He wondered if it was always the same time of day around here. And if he could even call it day.

Suddenly he realized that he needed to go to the bathroom. Did a magical house in a magical land have something so mundane as plumbing? His last request had been to contact his sister and he was put to sleep for his troubles. It was probably asking too much for there to be a telephone. But a bathroom was different!

As he jumped off the very comfortable bed, noticing that he still wore his shoes, a dreadful thought struck him. Maybe magical places had never needed to develop much in the way of technology. What if Mrs. Norse had an outhouse instead?

Or even worse, it could be that none of the denizens of this place needed a bathroom at all. That would explain the lack of catbox odors! Saving the Seasons and restoring his family and finding Fay would simply have to wait until he'd settled this more pressing matter.

At least there hadn't been any dreams, as she promised. The living room was empty. He could hear voices from the back yard. Before joining them, it wouldn't hurt to reconnoiter the terrain. Maybe he'd find what he needed by going through the kitchen.

The kitchen was nothing like the rest of the house but was the first really other-worldly attraction. Several blue globes, of various sizes, hung in space over the floor. Otherwise it was an empty room. He wondered where the food had come from, and the plates and silverware. Quite obviously, she had to extract these things from the globes ... or the globes made all the goodies appear somehow.

Of a dead certainty was that he would not be going to the bathroom in here, even if there were globes meant for such a function. He'd hate to get kitchen and bathroom globes mixed up!

His bladder was talking to him now. He had to do something quickly. That's when he noticed the lavender colored door off in a corner. He hadn't noticed it before. As he stepped through it and found all the modern conveniences, he had a strange feeling of *déjà vu*. The pink cover slip on the toilet reminded him of one he'd seen the time he visited Aunt Miner, the sort of touch he'd expect in an old lady's house ... but not in Mrs. Norse's!

When he finished and was washing his hands under an ornate faucet, he seemed to remember that very fixture once belonged to the grandparents on his father's side. His sudden suspicion that what he saw before him might be taken from his own mind and made real for his benefit did not cheer him even a little bit. He felt a cold shiver instead.

Hurrying back through the kitchen without looking back, his elbow bumped one of the spheres. It felt like a water balloon. He didn't want it to burst.

What a relief to step outside! The cats were in a semi-circle around Mrs. Norse. Wolf came running over and jumping on him the way he used to do when he was a puppy. A wave of good will flowed over Clive.

He couldn't help noticing a lawn mower, fire engine red, just beyond the cats. The very green lawn stretched out beyond this mower, stretched and stretched, and tilted upward until it disappeared in the distance. He'd never been in a backyard so large that you couldn't see the end of it.

Birds were singing way off somewhere, as if to celebrate the eternal, perfect day, with blue sky and green grass dividing the universe. "Now that you're rested, I hope you'll perform a small task," said Mrs. Norse, sounding more musical than the birds.

"Ma'am, I don't mean to seem ungrateful, but you said you'd put me in touch with my sister. That's what your strange book promised."

"Yes, Clive, and you want answers to all your questions."

"I know it's not your fault we're here. Granddad, or what he has become, is to blame."

"He does not share the blame alone, dear."

"I also know you have your own reasons for what you're doing." He made the comment somewhat testily but she nodded as if there could be no doubt as to the truth of his observation.

"As do we all, dear."

In a situation where one side held all the cards, and the other side didn't even know the rules of the game, there was only one sane course of action — especially in an insane world. Clive surrendered to the inevitable.

"You have something you wanted me to do," he said, eyeing

the lawn mower.

"Yes, I'd appreciate your mowing the lawn."

She sounded so reasonable. The only trouble was that the grass was already cut.

Chapter Thirteen
Who Sets The Rules

zzzzzzzzzzzzzzzzzzzzzzzzzzzzzzzzzzzzzzzzzplop!

Fay heard a man fishing with an expensive rod and reel. Emerging from behind one of the structures in which the Klave turtles explored relationships on the half shell, she saw a larger body of water than had been visible before. It was a perfect circle, the same as the ponds in which the turtles swam, but the water was a richer shade of blue.

At first she couldn't see the fisherman. Only part of his line and a yellow plastic floater came into view as she walked the circle. Odd clumps of the grey material (she still remembered how much she disliked the taste) were all over the place, some of the mounds as high as six feet. The fisherman stood behind one.

Everyone in Fay's party was walking casually in the same direction. She assumed that it was all right she was sort of out in front. She saw the man first. He was pale and thin, with a sunken chest and a posture that did nothing to flatter what was good in his features. Dark circles under his eyes completed the effect. He looked more skeletal in his own way than did the Tabriks.

"Hello!" boomed the hearty voice of Mr. Wynot. "Why if it isn't good old Mr. Brine, Assistant Treasurer to Mrs. Norse." Fay wondered if there were any people in this peculiar world besides important personages. There seemed to be an actual population of Tabriks, but when it came to normal looking humans — and normal animal life, for that matter — it was a very underpopulated environment. She'd started missing the variety of rich odors that she had taken for granted back home.

"Look what he's wearing!" shrieked Jennifer, pointing a trembling finger at a white button on the lapel of the double- breasted jacket that hung about his narrow frame. Mr. Wynot and the others seemed just as upset.

"Oh dear," commented the man, putting down his fishing equipment. His hand went to the button on which could be seen one lonely mark in jagged black lines: the letter **M**.

"The symbol of the evil one," moaned the Tabrik leader.

Mr. Brine removed the button and replaced it, only now it was quite different. He'd turned it around so that it showed the letter: **W**. In a flustered voice, Mr. Brine stuttered, "I - I'm sti- still wearing one of your campaign but-buttons, Mr. Wynot." Then he got hold of himself. "Please forgive my carelessness."

Everyone immediately relaxed, except Fay. The more she was around these people, the more they started seeming like adults from the old homeworld. Little kids gave her a pain, but nothing frustrated her more than the way grownups (or however they styled themselves) could go completely crazy over absolutely nothing.

Feeling a rubbing against her leg, she looked down at Kitnip who winked at her! She hadn't known that cats could wink.

"I know how you feel," said the cat. "I always know when you're tense like this. Except that how you feel right now is how I feel about all humans … most of the time."

Jennifer, smiling prettily, entered the fray. "Oh, I'm so embarrassed," she said. "What must you think of us."

"What's this all about?" asked Wynot.

"It's my fault," said Brine. "I'm always making stupid mistakes. My wife says I'm the greatest fool who ever lived, and that I never behave properly, and that I apologize too much. I know it's stupid when I start apologizing for my apologies, but somehow I can't help myself. And then…." He sighed at this point, paying no attention to the surprised expressions surrounding him. "There's nothing left to do but go fishing."

Mr. Wynot removed his helmet and wiped his brow. Fay was sure that if there'd been a sun in the sky he would have taken this opportunity to squint at it. "Now, now," he began, "I'm always interested in hearing about other people's domestic difficulties. Gives me a better perspective on how fortunate I am with dear old Mrs. Wynot. We get on splendidly. Of course, we only see each other every full rotation of the cosmos, but absence makes the heart grow fonder and all that. Still and all, before I lose everyone's attention, I should like to ask you, dear sir, just what is it you characterize as your fault?"

"The button!" observed Jennifer. "We've all behaved badly just now, and I'm to blame for starting it."

Fay laughed. "Well, it seems a big fuss over getting a letter of the alphabet upside down. It's only a black mark on a white circle, after all."

Kitnip meowed. Before the cat ever spoke in clear sentences, she had shown a knack for mimicking human speech, using shorter and longer sounds, and a rising emphasis that for all the world seemed like a asking a question. She made cat sounds rarely enough in this world that Fay took it as a very personal message to herself.

Fay bent down, and listened to the cat's advice: "Perhaps you should drop this subject, Fay. I seem to remember our world has nothing to brag about. People kill each other over symbols, instead of something reasonable like food and shelter. Once I remember how your father nearly foamed at the mouth when he saw a teenager on a motorcycle wearing a T-shirt that had a white circle with a few black marks on it."

"My goodness," remarked Fay. She could think of nothing else to say.

There is no telling how long this conversation might have gone on had they not had their attention distracted by something far more interesting than an exercise in polemics. A red cloud appeared out of nowhere and began heading in their direction. Remembering the cloud that Malak had sent against them on the stone mountain, Fay was afraid that he was launching another attack. She began to run when Jennifer reached out and caught her by the arm.

"It's all right," said Jennifer, "it's not what you think."

The cloud fell upon them ... except that it was not a cloud after all. Thousands of ladybirds surrounded them, tickling their arms and faces as they brushed past them. And all that Fay could think of was how just a short time before she had been wondering over the dearth of animal life in the Land of the Seasons.

"My goodness!" she said again, and this time with more feeling. The last of the birds fluttered away. They were identical to the terrestrial variety.

"I've got a great idea," said Jennifer. Let's go for a little dip." She began removing her dress.

"I don't have a bathing suit," said Fay.

"What's a bathing suit?" asked Jennifer, whose remarkable grasp of the English language and its rich vocabulary had failed her for the first time in her acquaintance with the girl from Earth.

"Uh, it's not important," muttered Fay, noticing that everyone else was starting to disrobe except for the Tabrik who didn't wear clothes. Although she hadn't given the matter a lot of thought before now, she found her eyes irresistibly drawn to the point on the Tabrik's body where the two legs met. Her curiosity was rewarded with much of nothing. She would refer to the Tabrik as an *it* except there was an ineffable male quality about him. All the Tabriks seemed identical. There was nothing remotely female about any of them.

But there was no question about the sexes of Mr. Wynot and Jennifer who seemed to be in a race to see who could take their clothes off the fastest. If she'd been asked one short week ago what would be one of her most important concerns after her parents disappeared, and she and her brother were dumped in another universe, she would not rank modesty very high on the list. Which only goes to show the limitations of self-knowledge.

She thought that when she had put her top back on, she

wouldn't have to go through this again. She started undressing, but very slowly. If she could only go slowly enough, maybe she could talk herself into it. When she was a little girl she hadn't minded taking her clothes off for baths or to change clothes no matter who was in the room.

Then had come a day when Mom put a firm stop to all that. Fay was surprised when she realized that Mom had been giving her little hints that she should start worrying about such matters. Fay wasn't much better at picking up on hints than Dad was about a million other things. At least at that time Fay had the excuse of being a little girl. Fathers didn't have excuses.

And speaking of excuses, Fay was going to have to come up with one or strip down with her new friends. She did want to go swimming. Folding her top, she placed it neatly on top of her bag, and then fumbled for the buttons on her shorts. Mr. Wynot in the nude didn't look much more ridiculous than he did with his clothes on. Jennifer was radiantly beautiful. Fay wondered if she would ever look that good. One could always hope.

Mr. Brine was still fishing. He put down his rod for a moment, removed his jacket, shook it out, then put it on again! Fay had the impression that the man was cold even though it was a warm.

"I'll finish up here in a moment," he said in a sad voice. "I don't want to be in your way. Besides, I must help the Tabriks count the latest harvest of Klaven eggs."

Fay was down to her panties, hoping for a last minute reprieve. Maybe she could go swimming like this. It wouldn't take long for them to dry out afterwards. She only hoped she wouldn't give offense for not going all the way.

If Dad were here, he'd be teasing her to join in the fun and be uninhibited. She realized that in this he was not typical of most fathers. Mom and he had enjoyed more arguments as a result. Claire was ten years younger than Russell, and had missed what he referred to in reverential tones as "The Sixties." Whenever he was in one of those moods, Mom would burst his balloon by throwing around one word: "Drugs." She said it non-reverentially.

Just thinking about her parents put a lump in Fay's throat. She remembered the feel and smell of her mother's hair after they'd shampooed together. She remembered helping look for one of Mom's contact lenses and how it looked like a drop of water in the white sink. She remembered Dad's aftershave lotion, Old Spice, and too many other things.

Better to forget, to think about anything else. Defiantly, she took off her panties and threw them with the rest of her clothes. It had to be coincidence what happened next.

The smooth surface of the water was broken by bubbles the size of small trailer homes. Simultaneously the fishing line went taut and almost pulled the rod from Mr. Brine's hands. Then something monstrous rose from the lake.

It was the biggest living thing Fay had ever seen, a cross between a fish and a spider, looming over all of them as if a construction project by an insane insect. The fishing line ended in the monster's jaws, dangling as if a thread. Kitnip hissed quite reasonably.

Grotesque as it looked, the worst part was how it moved — by inhaling tons of air through its horribly gasping mouth and then circulating the air through its long legs that were hollow. The whooshing sound set up a high pitched squeal that made Fay's ears feel like they were about to burst. She clasped her hands over her ears but she couldn't shut out the terrible sound.

Then the monster began to move. The air funnelled out through the legs, churning the water beneath the abomination. There was something very odd about seeing something that size actually hovering over the water. Then it began to run right at them.

Screaming, Mr. Brine threw down his fishing rod and fled with an awkward gait not much more graceful than the monster. The others were rooted to the spot, staring dumbfounded at the sight.

"We've got to make something to fight it," shouted the Tabrik leader, squatting down and plunging his long, delicate hands into one of the gray mounds of slimy material that studded the beach.

"Are you crazy?" cried Mr. Wynot, his white belly flopping as he grabbed at this clothes. They were all coming out of their trance of terror as the cause grew nearer. "There's no time! Only Mrs. Norse or Malak could activate the special substance quickly enough!"

Fortunately for all concerned, Kitnip kept her head ... and whiskers. "Use the special pine cones," she said to Fay.

"Always listen to cats in emergencies," agreed Jennifer, rushing over to help Fay who was already opening the sack.

"Wish I had hands," said Kitnip. Many the time Fay had thought the cat did have a pair she kept hidden somewhere — especially when she'd open doors.

Fay and Jennifer threw their first two cones in perfect unison. The spiny missiles curved upward in a graceful arc and connected with the target at almost the same moment.

The explosions were gratifyingly spectacular: KA-BLAAAAAM and PAH-BOOOOOOOOOM!

The monster answered with a sound of its own: sssssssssssssssssRRRRRRRRREEEEEEEEEEEEEEEEEEEEEEEEEEEEEEEEEEEE!

The only drawback to this cacophony was that the monster kept on coming, putting Fay in mind of a landlord with an eviction notice. What she really hated was that she was screaming and couldn't seem to stop. Jennifer was already grabbing for a new cone and Fay recovered enough to do the same.

Jennifer's bomb seemed to fall short of the target, but this time did more damage than the previous explosions against the main body of the thing. The new explosion was near one of the legs and succeeded in throwing the monster off balance. As it tipped forward, the head became a better target and Fay connected with it on her next try. No more pine cones were needed after that.

But as is so often the case, victory is rarely neat. The monster was still moving from remaining air in the legs after Fay had removed its head. And the carcass was still headed straight for them.

The girls ran for safety not a moment too soon as the spider-fish cracked up on shore. The cracking sounds it made were like a combination of splintering lumber and ripping rubber. It didn't smell very nice either. (At last Fay could appreciate some new odors.)

Fay's heart was beating so fast that she could hardly catch her breath. Jennifer was breathing hard, too, and gasping out short little sounds that turned out to be words when Fay's breathing slowed down sufficiently so that she could listen again.

"I told ... you ... those cones ... should only ... be used...."

"Against monsters," Fay finished.

"Yuck," observed Kitnip.

Jennifer helped Fay to stand and she again noticed they were both naked. In the heat of excitement, she had completely forgotten.

"Do we go swimming now?" asked Fay, laughing. Jennifer responded by playfully pushing her in the direction of the water.

"Oh, Mr. Brine?" came Mr. Wynot's voice from behind one of the grayish mounds.

"Yes," came a quivering voice from behind yet another mound.

"You'll be able to tell everyone you caught a big one today."

Meanwhile, in a black fortress hidden between two snow covered cliffs deep in the heart of Winter, Malak, the Dour One, observed all that had recently transpired in the domain of Spring. He was dressed in purple robes, in the manner of the ancient Caesars of Earth, except the material of his clothing was woven of a much warmer material. It was a really smart outfit.

The way he kept up with all Four Seasons, and his home world as well, was by means of television sets; and video recorders for when he couldn't schedule the time to see a certain event contemporaneously. But as he had just caused the visitation of the water monster, he watched that one live.

"Yes, dear Fay," he said to the flickering screen, "I'll get you, my granddaughter, and your little cat, too!"

One of his slaves nodded so vigorously that a thin line of drool fell from his mouth onto a copy of *The Book of the Seasons*, the same book that Mrs. Norse had shown Clive. There were only two copies of the book in all existence. They were identical in all respects except that Lord Malak's copy now had an itty bitty little stain of saliva at the exact center of the silver design on the cover.

There was enough of Grandfather's mind left, at least enough of the French side, to deeply regret waste. The little creature that had just drooled on his most cherished possession had required time and effort to create. He Who Was Malak thought about the effort he'd put into the little creature — he really did — as he rubbed at the wet spot on the cover of his copy of *The Book of the Seasons*. He watched the wet spot become larger. His eyebrow went up, the way it always did when he was trying to exercise self control, as a little bit of silver thread came a wee bit loose on his book.

Malak turned and took a good, long look at the four foot high homunculus. The little guy was of the same design as the jack-'o-lantern men of Autumn. Only the grey material-of-making had a completely different texture here in Winter. The head was blue-grey, as if a snowman's head. The little fella hadn't been nearly as much trouble to make as the copy Malak had made of himself. Now that had been hard work, but he destroyed it anyway just to make a dramatic point with the old taking-the-head-off-and-throwing-it routine. The first nightmare Clive ever had was inspired by the Disney cartoon version of "The Legend of Sleepy Hollow," and Malak couldn't waste that knowledge.

Still, it was one thing to destroy for a purpose and another to destroy out of spite. He carefully weighed his options and made a decision.

"Hey there," he said, putting his arm around the creature, "I should get around to giving all of you names someday. How'd you like to be called Droopy or Grumpy or Snoopy or Snuffy, eh?"

The little guy looked up in awe at his maker and produced a touch more drool. This was not a speaking model.

"Have you performed any useful tasks for me lately?" The creature nodded. These beings were incapable of lying so Malak knew he'd gotten some use out of the thing. And there's no doubt that it would have been more cost effective to repair the defective mouth than lead its owner over to the window with a splendid view of icy wasteland under stark blue sky ... and then push the little fellow out into the abyss.

"There's something to be said for spite," said Malak to the stark scenery marking his domain.

Grandfather would never deliberately throw anything away. Nor was the original Malak a natural spendthrift as he was still using certain rocks as paperweights, all that remained of early opponents. But Malak was vindictive in ways that Grandfather could never approach. The more time anyone donned the guise of Malak, the more Malak he became.

"That bitch Norse can't change the rules," he said to the vault of heaven. "She knows it and I know it. Just because she's defeated me every other time doesn't mean history, or her story, will be the same this time! I only have to win one time to get what I want. She has to win every time and that will prove her undoing."

To a casual observer flying by the castle tower, it might seem that Malak was talking to himself. In actuality, he was addressing a tremendous pile of the grey stuff out of which both he and his nemesis could create living beings. A lot had gone into making the spider-fish, a complete washout. Even before his hand touched it, the material possessed a rudimentary consciousness, pulsating and trembling at every word.

Then again, maybe he was talking to himself. "Rome wasn't built in a day, and a perfect hatred takes tender loving care," he continued speaking to the quivering sludge. "My stupid daughter and her no good husband were on the way to a perfect divorce. They followed all the steps: love replaced by indifference, indifference mutates into intolerance, intolerance bubbles and boils until passion returns, only now we have hate instead of love. Out of their negative energy will my dreams come true!"

For a moment, Malak was almost happy. He went over to one of the television monitors and brought up a picture of Mr. Gurney lying on his stomach in the wheat field where the poor man had collapsed from exhaustion. An ugly looking sunburn covered his naked back. Malak let himself enjoy the picture, but just for a moment because he didn't want to become hooked on the boob tube.

After congratulating himself on putting Dad in a world with a sun in the sky, Malak brought up a picture of Mom. She was sitting on the ground, leaning against one of the semi-transparent walls. The little male figures continued jumping up and down outside the radius of the walls. They would never grow tired, although their duration was not forever. Eventually they would simply disappear as they burned up from their exertions. By that point, she would have so internalized them that their physical presence would no longer be required.

Then he decided to tune in Clive and Fay. He gave them both a cursory glance. Fay had recovered from the attack. Clive was safe with Mrs. Norse. He couldn't make up his mind what to do about the kids. He had a few options, based on one simple requirement: the young Gurneys must be turned to his advantage so that Norse would regret bringing them here ahead of schedule.

He turned back to his gray pile of sludge and began kneading the edges. As he worked, he resumed his soliloquy, enjoying the squishing feeling of the muddy gook between his fingers: "Where Mrs. Norse will make her mistake is in assuming I'll employ the same approach I've used every other time, trying to make one season obliterate the rest while maintaining its original character. Besides, she expects I have a preference for Winter to win."

There didn't seem to be any talking creations around to help out at this point so he had to keep the ball rolling himself: "Ah, but isn't that so, you might ask? Don't I want Winter to win? That used to be true ... but not any longer! Here, let me demonstrate."

Malak had been living alone for a long time and had come to rely on himself for company. The fact that he incorporated different people in himself was a big help.

After wiping his hands, he produced a fresh leaf from inside his cloak, where it had remained unaltered since he picked it in Summer. As he held it up to the window, he concentrated on the beauty of its design. The leaf trembled in his hand, and then went through all the metamorphoses of its life cycle: from healthy green, to orange and gold as life slowly ebbed from it, to a brown caricature of its original vitality ... and then it was a frost covered outline, turning to powder, as if all the cold outside Malak's castle had been thrust into the heart of the leaf.

Malak talked some more: "That's what I can do now. But when I'm through with my great experiment, the next leaf will undergo a fifth state of existence, completely different from its condition in the Four Seasons." He laughed in a manic way that Grandfather would never have done even if he did laugh!

"The Fifth Season is my great invention, not at all what Norse and her stooges expect. And after I take care of them, we'll see about bringing back the night."

He looked out the window at the blue patch of sky. "Night for all the universes." He wasn't laughing now.

"Forever."

Chapter Fourteen
Questing Around

"I won't fall back in love with you!" Mother's voice addressed his father from months ago, captured and released again to renew Clive's pain. He'd eavesdropped on that particular argument. He knew Mom was talking to Dad. But hearing it again, ripped from its original context, he felt that she talked to him.

"Mother?" he asked of the sky. Or had the sounds come from the great green expanse that was Mrs. Norse's back yard? It was as green and flat as a pool table, stretching out farther than the eye could see with a perfectly kept row of hedges on the right, and a white stone wall on the left, both stretching to the horizon.

"Bad memories are like germs, waiting to reinfect the unwary" said Mrs. Norse. "Clive, you don't have to mow the lawn if you don't want to. But I think you'll find it's just what you need, and the grass could use it."

His mother's words had shaken him badly. The only benefit he could derive was redoubling his desire to rescue his parents, to save them from dangers … and perhaps from themselves.

But as she had done before, Mrs. Norse seemed to read his mind. "You're in a good position to achieve reunion with your family, Clive, but not if you try too hard! There is a rule of indirection you should observe. If you try to achieve your heart's desire by a direct approach, you will fail."

"One of your rules, I'll bet!" he snapped.

She was annoyingly calm as always: "Real rules set themselves. They are the basis of Natural Law. False rules aren't rules but lies, the laws of Malak and his State."

Wolf came over and licked his hand. Clive could be back home as far as that went because the dog hadn't said a word since he'd come out into the back yard. *Mine is not to reason why, mine is to cut the grass,* he thought. If she wanted him to do this, there must be a reason. But the lawn was already so neatly trimmed that the idea seemed preposterous. *Oh well, mine's not to reason why....*

He gave the lawnmower a thorough going-over. It wasn't the old fashioned model he would have expected, the kind with blades in a spiral that turn only with an unseemly exertion of muscle power. It was a power motor, but with a cord instead of a switch. The only item missing was the gas tank.

He could feel the smile in Mrs. Norse's words: "It doesn't require fuel."

Looking at the seemingly infinite vista of lawn, he could only shrug. There would never be enough fuel for all that anyway. How long he would hold out was anyone's guess, but he'd be good for twice as long with grass that didn't need cutting! He was only sure of one fact: the sooner he started, the sooner he could stop thinking about it.

Yanking the cord, he found it only took one try for the lawnmower to sputter to life. Real life, that is. The motor purred as though a hundred cats were inside, all in unison the way the cats had done earlier. He could feel the handlebars throb under his grasp as if blood coursed through them. Wolf made a slight whining at what could not be a pleasant experience for him.

"It won't talk, will it?" Clive asked.

Mrs. Norse laughed. The largest Persian there commented, "That would be ridiculous."

Wolf chose this moment to express an opinion: "Hey, the kid doesn't know. He's still getting over listening to me yap. I wouldn't be surprised to hear anything talk around here."

"Thanks, Wolf," said Clive, feeling better as he took the mower out of neutral and started his chore, his task, his impossible labor.... The mower moved quite easily as was to be expected with no thickness of grass underneath. The object was to see how long it would take to reach the end of the lawn so he could turn around and come back. Drifting over to the hedges, he had the notion that he might as well do the job in straight lines, starting on the right side and going up and down until he was against the wall opposite.

The mower wasn't the kind that pulled you along. He had to push, but that was no problem. Except that as he proceeded, the grass was becoming imperceptibly thicker. A very little spray of green was coming out of the mower at last. He was glad that she didn't use a bag to catch each blade.

He hadn't mowed any grass recently except when Dad asked him to do the family yard. That was a lot harder than this. First of all, there were all the trees and bushes to go around. Dad didn't do the best job of keeping all the branches trimmed, but he didn't trust Clive or Fay to manicure his beloved greenery. Inevitably, Clive would come in from the yard covered in scratches.

Then Mom would fuss over him and get out the bandaids and ointments. He hardly noticed the scratches but what he hated about working in the yard was that he'd pick up insect bites. He never noticed getting them at the time but suddenly they'd be all over his arms and legs — big, ugly welts itching like crazy.

Now as he pushed the red lawn mower up the incredible length of Mrs. Norse's backyard, he concluded that what he liked best about this world was the apparent lack of insects. At least he hadn't seen any yet. Whether or not he would count something like the monster that had attacked Fay was an open question.

For a moment, he thought he saw an insect flitting at the periphery of his vision; but he turned his head quickly to see that it was a speck of yellow pollen floating on the air. As he watched, it drifted down and touched the grass a few feet to the left of where he was mowing. As it made contact, there was a little pop as of a soap bubble bursting.

Again he heard his mother's voice: "We try to be fair to both of you but it's not Fay's fault that she's a better student than you are."

God, he'd almost succeeded in making himself forget that conversation, but now old memories, sharper than a wasp's sting, came drifting down out of cool Autumn air. Where was all this stuff coming from? Maybe he could follow the "pollen" to its source. Another landed with its load of joy from Dad: "You're not very good, son." At least his parents had been able to agree on something.

The grass was finally growing thick enough to require some effort on his part. The whole lawn was subtly tilting upward, making it harder to just push the mower along. Added to this was the unpleasant prospect of more pollen drifting into view, always coming from in front of him. Another popped and he heard Dad's voice again, but discoursing on a different subject: "A man needs one place in this lousy world where he can be as big a jerk as he wants and not pay a price." Clive had never heard that one before, but all he could think was that Dad was a jerk to talk that way.

The next one popped and it was Mom again: "You don't treat me like a real person! You're as sensitive as an episode of Championship Wrestling." He didn't remember Mom ever making jokes when she and Dad argued, but maybe that was something she reserved for rare private moments. Clive wondered why if wives thought it was so important that husbands treat them with respect that they didn't set a better example in how they regarded their children. Personhood was apparently a restricted commodity.

Subversive thoughts were interrupted by half a dozen of the small yellow timebombs coming to rest right in front of the lawnmower. Mom and Dad's angry voices were intermingled and chopped up along with the grass. He grabbed the control on the mower and put it on maximum. Now he was looking for more of the pollen so he could run it over. Grandfather must be behind this, seeding the sky with malice.

The ground tilted up again, and he had to start pushing really hard to keep it going forward. He could feel the pressure in his wrists and it was harder to get traction. There was pollen up ahead, but he couldn't get to it in time to stop from hearing new torments. First, there was Dad saying: "I swear I'll never lose my temper like that again. You have my word."

Then there was Mom saying, "I know I promised I'd never leave you, but there comes a time when you have to face that it's over. You need to get on with your life!"

Clive shouted, "Shut up, both of you!" He was louder than the mower, louder than the hollow words from the past, louder than all the promises ever made. He turned the mower off and collapsed on the soft grass, still telling the blue sky with its flecks of yellow to leave him alone. Other pollen was drifting all around him.

It didn't seem that he'd been mowing that long, but he was already out of sight of the house. There was nothing behind him but a vast sea of green and the gigantic totem pole, so tall that it seemed to hold up the sky. As the voices started up again, he decided to get back to work, if only in hope that the purring noise would drown out yesterday's recriminations. Everything was Mom and Dad criticizing and accusing, finding fault with everyone and everything, as if some manic editor had sifted out every fine thought and sentiment they'd ever had, leaving only the bile.

Starting up the mower again, he regretted that it wasn't noisy enough to overwhelm the talk, talk, talk; but there were so many random sentences flying around that they succeeded in obliterating each other's meaning. The saving grace of too much carping was that it changed itself into white noise.

The mowing was becoming harder and this distracted his attention, as well. The exertion produced thick drops of perspiration on his brow. Wiping his head with the back of his hand, he felt dull pain in his ankles as he pushed up an ever steeper incline. He was just about to call it quits when the mower slipped out of his hands and started rolling back toward him. Grabbing for the handle, he only succeeded in knocking the machine on its side, where it skidded a few feet before coming to a stop.

He felt sick when he saw what was underneath. The mower had no blade but rather what appeared to be several rows of teeth and fangs. He wanted to quit and just walk away from his "chore," but he wasn't about to defy Mrs. Norse at this stage. Besides, he was curious about just how much longer it would take to reach the end of the lawn. From the top of the stone mountain, he hadn't been able to see as far into Autumn as his current location. He was dying to see more.

The grass was very high now and the pollen was still drifting up ahead. When he lost his footing, he grabbed at the green tendrils and they supported his weight. At least the mower wasn't drifting back. Perhaps the teeth were holding on as desperately as he was. Craning his neck, he could see what might to be the end of the lawn, a great mound of weed covered earth, beyond which was the blue of heaven. He dreaded that it might only be the top of a hill with another vista of grass beyond, but he was encouraged that it would at least be downhill if he could reach that point.

He hurried the rest of the way and stopped as he reached the summit. Catching his breath, he looked over the edge. Only there was no edge, only an unbroken surface of more grass descending and gathering itself into a huge ball that hung out in space beyond where the wall and hedge terminated, as if sliced off by a giant cleaver. Below the ball was yellow mist, the same mist he had witnessed in his vision, that Fay had seen in her dream, that was the distant fog they'd both seen from the stone mountain. The yellow pollen was drifting up from the mist, yellow dots separating themselves from yellow space.

While he was contemplating this new marvel, another problem reared its head... literally. The huge mound that seemed to hang in space began to move. It lifted itself up and the piece of earth on which he clung shifted and moved as well. Then the ball turned and faced him.

He was looking into the blazing red eyes of a dragon. There was no doubt about it. Just because the monster was covered in grass instead of scales didn't make it any less of a dragon. As the leviathan opened its jaws wide, he saw gigantic teeth that didn't resemble in the least your standard lawn features.

There was a morbid fascination in staring at a dragon, the same nervous excitement a bird experiences in the presence of a snake — a prickly skin feeling that goes along with the idea you may be someone's next meal. Fortunately, the yawning abyss of the jaws came no closer but swung back and forth as the creature spoke.

"Why have you stopped the treatment?" it asked.

"Hello," Clive responded stupidly.

"It felt so good, the trim you were giving me. Uh oh, you better stand back, I'm going to sneeze."

Clive wouldn't have known any greater terror at that moment if he'd been told he was going to be eaten instead. Fortunately, the dragon turned his head. The sneeze had the force of an earthquake, and that's what it was. Clive hung on to the weeds, or whatever they were, for dear life, as the sticky wind escaped the dragon's nostrils, releasing the odor of damp earth and roots.

"That's better," said the dragon. Clive saw more yellow pollen in the air, drifting up from the fog below, and obviously the cause of the leviathan's sneeze. "The trouble maker's still making trouble," lamented the dragon.

"You mean my grand... I mean, Malak," Clive corrected himself.

"He wants to screw up my environment, yank the chain on my eco systems, and give me a hard time in general."

"He hates dragons?" Clive let himself use the word, but he felt nervous about it. He'd used the word dwarf around a dwarf at a state carnival and let himself in for a speech about how little people didn't like the term. He'd called Fay a girl at school and received a lecture from one of the teachers, Miss Mims, about the unadvisability of that term. For all he knew, "dragon" might be considered a pejorative in this neighborhood.

The dragon didn't mind being called a dragon. He did, however, suggest a problem having to do with plurals as opposed to singulars. "Hey kid, let me clue you: there is only one dragon. All else are reflections of myself. If I get sick, then your Earth dragon comes down with a bellyache, too, and your seasons are adversely affected — but as I say, the Earth dragon is just another extension from the old sod."

This was not what Clive expected to hear from a dragon, but then he'd never expected to be engaging in conversation with an ambulatory lawn. He pictured dragons in caves where they guarded hordes of treasure and ate princesses when hungry for a snack. He couldn't imagine this dragon doing anything so uncouth but wondered over its relationship with Mrs. Norse, besides sharing her most annoying trait: the mind reading business.

"I only collect real treasure," it said, "what grows and dies with the changes of Life. But I know what you want to see: fierce looking swords with jewel encrusted hilts..."

"Well, I..." Clive began.

"Or an Egyptian sarcophagus covered in gold and silver, or a Roman bowl of exquisite workmanship, or a Viking's sturdy helmet with maybe a touch of dried blood on the horns..."

"How is that you ..." Clive began again.

"Or a Persian warrior's burnished shield, or Sumerian goblets and arm rings, or diamonds which are a girl's best friend, or how about American Express traveler's checks — don't leave home without them..."

"I get the idea," said Clive.

"Sorry about that. My Lady didn't send you to me just so I'd have a captive audience. You were doing a favor for me, and I'm supposed to do something for you."

"Like what?"

"Didn't you want something a short time ago?"

Clive felt like a ripe idiot. Here Mrs. Norse was trying to help him in her subtle way but he was too dumb to notice. For all he knew, he was talking to the most powerful being he would ever meet. Time for a wish!

"I want to be with my sister again."

"You got it."

"And I want to save my parents."

"That's harder, because they have a say in their own salvation, but I can help you try. Anything else?"

How many wishes did he have? The traditional three? Or was it unlimited? Should he ask for riches? A lack of money had been the root of much evil back home. Should he ask for wisdom? If he had that, he could solve other problems that would come his way. And there was good health to consider, but he couldn't rightly ask for that without including the rest of his family.

He forgot that the dragon could read minds: "Excuse me for interrupting this exercise in megalomania, kid, but when I asked if there was anything else, it was a figure of speech, you know. You're in this world now, and you have to deal with these problems. If you ask me, your whole family could use a lesson in the importance of the here and now."

"Leave them out of this," said Clive, feeling stupider than ever. There must be a limit to how many times you could defy a dragon before he put you on the menu.

Amazingly, the dragon apologized: "I take it back for one member of your family, only. Fay has her head screwed on straight. And I think it is time you were with her again so you may benefit from her good example."

And with that, the dragon suddenly lowered its head so suddenly that Clive lost his hold and fell straight into the yellow fog. He was prepared to scream all the way down ... but once he was in the fog, he didn't seem to be falling anymore. Rather, he was experiencing a floating sensation. This lasted for a long time and he became used to it.

He was not alone in the fog, not exactly. Thanks to free floating pollen, Mom and Dad's voices continued to bedevil him. Only now they were not selections from the past but an amalgam of both giving him a hard time: "So you're having a big adventure," the dual voice taunted him, "but how long will it be before you start to stink? You didn't bring any deodorant along, now did you? No change of clothes? No toothbrush? First your underarms will reek and you didn't even bring chewing gum to fight bad breath. Then the perspiration will dry from all your exertions, such as mowing the grass, and every square inch of your skin will have a nasty, musty odor, that will seep into your clothes. We're just as glad you're not home but floating around. If you were home, you'd take a shower instead of a bath and you always let the water run too long, and too hot. You were never frugal with water or with anything else. Every spot of mildew in the bathroom was your fault. We never should have had you. Who can afford children today? Fay wasn't much better, but at least she didn't drain our hard earned money as quickly you did, you ungrateful...."

Fortunately, he didn't have to listen to more. He was rescued by the sound of crashing surf and a salt water taste in the air. He plunged into the cold, bracing waters of an ocean like nothing he'd yet seen in the Land of the Seasons. Floundering around in the rolling waves was just what he needed to wash away dirt from his body and ... his mind. He felt refreshed and clean.

An unintended gulp of sea water brought him up, coughing. His eyes were smarting from the salt. He was grateful to be near a rocky coastline and swam for it, wishing he was as good at this as his sister. Not until he'd pulled himself on shore did he notice the big surprise.

It was late afternoon, sunlight making a million sparkling diamonds on the slowly rippling ocean. Sunlight. There was a gold-red sun, hanging low, streaking the sky with color. And if he was somewhere where there was a sun, did this mean he was back on earth?

Nearby there was one sickly tree, bereft of leaves, covered in leprous, black bark. All the naked branches were reaching to his right. The sea was to his left. The constant wind blowing in from the sea had swept across this tree every day until it grew at this angle. It seemed to be pointing in the direction he would inevitably take: there was only one path, one sign of human presence — what he hoped was a human presence.

An old woman was hobbling up the path. Perhaps she could help him. Taking a deep breath, Clive felt the brine penetrate to his sinuses. As she drew near, he noticed the spiderweb cracks that covered her face as if some old, oil painting had come to life, and opened a grinning, toothless mouth with which to speak.

"Hello," said Clive.

"About time," she said in a high pitched voice. Then the old crone laughed with a hideous cackle.

"Do I know you?" Clive asked, still rubbing the sea from his eyes.

"I should think you'd recognize your own sister," spat the crone. "I'm Fay!"

Chapter Fifteen
The Shunning

What a revoltin' development! He didn't remember where he'd heard that phrase but it came back to him now like a wet fish slapped across his face. "I don't believe it," he sputtered. "You're not Fay."

The old crone cackled again. "Oh, no? How about the time I put chocolate syrup in your underpants? Heh, heh, heh."

He blinked. That's about all he could manage. He blinked some more. Maybe, just maybe, this decrepit wreck of a human being was what Fay might become one day — if she never had the benefits of medical science, a good diet, shopping malls, air conditioning, makeup, facelifts, social security checks, greeting cards sent for every possible occasion, endless phone calls from friends and her children and grandchildren, a convenient husband somewhere along the way who could be put out to pasture or otherwise disposed of when the time was right, vitamins, supplements, subscriptions to *Reader's Digest,* investments (especially mutual funds), mudpacks, beauty parlors, aerobics, courses in self-esteem, group therapy, sit coms, female hygiene products and a rewarding career. But despite all that, Clive had his doubts this was really Fay.

"Well, do you recognize me?" asked the old woman. "Your mind seemed to be wandering."

"You leave my mind out of this," he said defensively. "Anyone could have known about the chocolate syrup. Maybe you captured Fay and tortured secrets out of her."

"Ha," said the old woman with contempt.

"Or maybe you're Malak in disguise, or Grandfather, that is. Yeah, that would make sense."

"Who sent you here?" she asked.

"Er, the dragon."

"Who sent you to the dragon?"

"Mrs. Norse."

"The good guys, kiddo. The good guys!" She was most emphatic on that point. "Why would they send you into the arms of Malak?"

Trying to trip him up on logic, was she? More evidence this was Fay ... but Grandfather was no slouch in noticing details about human beings caught in his net. Clive wanted proof.

"OK, you're either Fay or one of Malak's creatures...."

"Slaks," she added helpfully.

"You've always had a better memory."

"Come on Clive, I'm remembering this stuff from over seventy years ago and it's just yesterday for you."

He blinked again. She was good, awfully good. The perversity of the situation fit in with everything else that had started to go wrong ever since the fateful day Granddad had taken them out on his damned lake. Clive had asked to see Fay. And now he was seeing Fay ... maybe.

"The last time I saw you," he began, "was a drawing of you with some strange people in the Land of Spring. Mrs. Norse showed me the drawing in her special book. I'd asked to see you and then...."

"I was never in Spring," she said. "The moment we were separated on the mountain of stone, Malak seized me and brought me here."

This was becoming complicated. Would Mrs. Norse have lied to him? Wouldn't a Malakian trick be likelier? "Then what happened?" he asked, all attention.

"Malak said he'd make me one of his tax collectors," said the crone. "He explained that magic could be broken down into small units and traded back and forth. He needed to collect a certain amount in order to perform a very powerful spell." As she recounted her story, Clive remembered how Malak had made the same spiel to Wolf and himself but elected to keep this information a secret for the time being. "At first I resisted," she concluded, "but when he put Mom and Dad's lives in my hands, I gave in. This was many years ago. You've just traveled through time."

"So they're dead now," he said, more to himself than to her.

She cackled again. He really hated that. "You'd think so," she said, "but I saved them in more ways than one. Now they're younger than I am, eternally young you might say. You can see for yourself!" Her claw-like hand reached out and took him by the arm. Her touch was loathsome but he didn't resist. Worse than her touch was the sour odor rising from her rags, some unholy combination of rotting fish and grapes.

She led him along the snaking path until they came upon a village of squat, grey cottages, worn from centuries of neglect. Although the denizens must take their life from the broad ocean, the cottages were turned away from the water, facing a barren cliffside. "This is the village, Il," she said.

"But wait ... " He hesitated to call her Fay. "If this is not the Land of the Seasons, where are we?"

"Another world, not Earth. A planet steeped in evil." She made a terrible gesture at the equally terrible houses. "Mom and Dad are now lords of ... this."

He dared not pursue the matter further, not until he'd learned something. At the seaside, this new environment had seemed liberating, as the sun in the sky had been reassuring. As they walked along the rough path into the village, however, the atmosphere seemed to change; the air grew heavy and stagnant. He began to feel a fear unlike anything he'd yet experienced.

"You pull away, dear brother," said the woman, digging her claws the more deeply into his arm. More and more he doubted her reality. But then two people emerged from the nearest cottage (a construction built so low that it seemed to be virtually part of the ground) whose identity he did not question.

"Mother?" he asked uncertainly. "Father?" he echoed himself. The duo were young and appeared healthy. Mom still had her raven dark hair and pale complexion. Dad was no longer balding but had regained his full head of sandy hair. They were dressed in black as though in mourning for themselves. Except that the plain, black garb was exotic and luxurious when viewed at close range, as Clive was in a position to witness. He broke free from the withered hand holding him and rushed forward to embrace his parents.

He hugged Mom and she didn't resist. But he felt the coldness beneath her clothes, as if she'd been disintered for this family reunion. As he pulled back he saw her immobile face, like a mask carved out of ice. He was still looking at her as he groped for his father, who pushed him away and held out his hand instead for a more formal exchange of greetings. Clive shuddered at the corpse-like coldness of that hand.

"Welcome home," screamed the old woman who claimed to be his sister. "You've come at just the right time."

Wondering how being nearly a century late could be considered punctual, Clive had to remind himself of the time frame described by old Fay. "Come with us, son," said Dad. "Today you'll be a man..."

"And do a man's work," Mom finished the thought. The crone cackled again and began shouting. She was surprisingly vocal for one of her advanced years. As she cried out, the doors to the cottages creaked open and the denizens of the Village Il emerged to greet the setting sun. The last cottage produced a little girl, all of nine years old.

"Oh, God," said Clive as he recognized Anne Jeffries, Fay's young friend who had been frightened so badly by the singing wall paper. She had her hands tied in front of her and was being led by a man who looked like her father. "Anne!" he called out.

She didn't recognize him at first, seeming to be in some kind of trance. Clive started toward her but Dad blocked him, arm held out straight against his son's chest. "Listen to me, Clive," he said. "You've been a disappointment up until now. This is your last chance to make me proud of you."

Dad could see the consternation and confusion playing tag across his son's face and placed his other hand on the young man's shoulder. "Don't speak to that girl again, you hear me? If you do, you're no son of mine."

Clive's mouth was open but absolutely nothing came out. Mom spoke for him: "She's been chosen, son, and we don't speak to those who are chosen."

Naturally that's when Anne noticed Clive and called out to him. But now old Fay's claw hand was at his back, and her insistent whispering reminded him to mind his parents. Anne called out once more but gave up after that. Her small body sagged when it was obvious that he could do nothing for her.

When about one hundred people had gathered, Dad gestured for everyone to follow him. Clive stumbled along beside his parents. Anne was brought up near the head of the procession as well, but a sidelong glance showed him that she was staring straight ahead, oblivious to everyone. The sun was just above the water, making two perfect circles, one rippling and the other steadfast, beckoning the people of Il on their way until the mob reached a small beach of pebbles and stones.

There was an ominous cave looking out onto a pool of brackish water that was left by the tide. There was a terrible stink coming out of that cave of long dead rotten things from the bottom of the deepest possible ocean. Suddenly a small knife was in Mom's hand and she went at Anne. Clive was about to lunge between his mother and the girl when he saw that all that was happening was the cutting of the child's ropes. Then Dad placed a hand on Clive's shoulder.

"Son, it's time for you to do what a son's gotta do."

"Uh, what's that, Pop?" asked Clive, casting furtive glances every which way. There must be some hope of escape for both

Anne and himself.

"It's your turn to collect the taxes," said Mom. "This child has defied proper authority, so first she is shunned, and then she is expelled from the community in a manner that will benefit the community."

"Uh huh," said Clive, still looking wildly for anything that might help. "So what do you want me to do?"

"Feed her to the Maw," said old Fay. "The friendly little critter inside that cave is one of Malak's pets. He receives magical energy every time the Maw feeds, and he lets us have the surplus for our own requirements at the local level."

Clive felt his head nodding and lips pulled back in a silly grin. These people couldn't possibly be his family. There was no way he could believe it. But how would he get out of this one? "So what does he give you?" he asked, stalling for time.

"Life extension, for one," said Dad.

"We can't do it for ourselves," said Mom, regretfully. "Only blood of our blood can provide us with the gift. But poor Fay is getting a bit old for the ritual."

"You know how much I've always loved them," said the old woman, cackling yet again. Clive kept on nodding. No doubt about it, they were not his family. Malak must be getting desperate if he thought Clive would fall for this song and dance.

"So what do I do?" asked Clive.

"Take this unwilling subject," said Dad, "drag her to the cave, call out the Maw, and throw her in its mouth."

"Oh, is that all?" asked Clive, but his hands were shaking. He hoped no one noticed. The eyes of the village Il were heavy upon him and he went to Anne who offered no resistance. Maybe the best strategy was to call out the monster and then not toss him the expected vittles. If he and the girl ran for it, the monster might be sufficiently peeved to attack the others.

Anne let him drag her to the edge of the cave, but then began struggling, albeit weakly, at the immediate prospect before her.

"Yoo hoo," Clive called out. "Oh, you in there, it's dinnertime." At first, there was nothing to see but white mist seeping out of the cave. Then it began to creep up Anne's body, slowly, inexorably, until thin tendrils of whiteness were reaching for her throat. The stench of the sea bottom was overwhelming.

Clive began seeing fragmentary details within the mist: a fin, a claw, a large red, glistening something — all part of a shape that was constantly shifting. One moment he thought he saw a metal surface; then it was fresh, wet scales; then the mist was of a different density. There were many eyes and a glimpse of wings. Everything was dreadfully still with no hint of a breeze. The only sound, besides the quickened breathing of Anne and himself, was the eager murmuring of the crowd. He hated them more than he did the insubstantial horror curling around his feet. Before little Anne disappeared into that mist, he had to act. Grabbing her narrow shoulders, he yanked her back and fell into the tidepool. The sudden silence of the crowd was mute testimony to his recklessness.

"Help!" he shouted to no one in particular as the amorphous entity swirled over his head. Holding Anne by the hand, he pulled her sideways and got them both to their feet. "Run," he told her.

"YOU SAID THE MAGIC WORD BUT YOU DON'T GET A RUBBER DUCK!" boomed the voice of the dragon from directly overhead.

"Huh, what?" he blubbered, still running past the people of Il who stood there as complacent as wax dummies, which characterization included his erstwhile family. "Magic word?"

"YOU CALLED FOR HELP."

Clive stopped running so quickly that Anne went ahead of him and did a pratfall because he hadn't let go of her hand. She lay there, unmoving. "You mean to say you would have let us die if I didn't say HELP?"

"NAH, YOU SAVED YOURSELF THE MOMENT YOU REFUSED TO ACTUALLY PERFORM THE SACRIFICE. AND

THERE'S NO ONE HERE TO DIE EXCEPT YOU!"

Clive scrutinized the little girl lying in the sand. Then he strolled over to the crowd and examined a few of them before he got really picky with Mom, Dad and one old crone whose family resemblance seemed considerably less convincing now. When the figures had been moving, they'd seemed genuine enough, just as the substitute Mom and Dad back on Earth could have passed with most anyone who knew them. It was just that when they were immobile, as they were now, the bodies seemed to have a slight, waxy quality that gave them away. Or at least he thought he had detected something new.

He really hated Slaks. And something else was bothering him. "Are you always this loud?" he asked. "It hurts to listen."

"ONLY WHEN I'M SENDING MESSAGES TO THE FAR REACHES OF THE SEASONS. THERE'S A LOT OF MALAK INTERFERENCE TO OVERCOME."

"The Seasons? Isn't this another planet?" No sooner had Clive asked the question than twilight evaporated. The sun blinked and he was staring into a colossal eyeball attached to a pair of wings that flapped ponderously against the sky. As for the Maw, its misty substance was undergoing a remarkable transformation as it literally condensed.

The roaring of the surf was becoming louder as the mist turned into stinking rain that hissed into the sand.

At least the ocean remained unchanged. "The Land of the Seasons is an island, right?" asked Clive of the sky. "We couldn't see this far from the mountain." He received no answer. "Hey, how do I get back?"

"QUESTIONS ABOUT GEOGRAPHY ARE OUT OF BOUNDS, NO PUN INTENDED. THIS TIME I'LL GET YOU TO YOUR SISTER, BUT LET'S TAKE ONE SMALL PRECAUTION AGAINST ANY MORE OF MALAK'S DETOURS. I DIDN'T REALLY EXPECT HIM TO GO THIS FAR."

The precaution consisted of Clive dipping his hands into the sand where the Maw had suffered dissolution, and then rubbing the damp and sticky grit on his face. He kept sand out of his eyes by holding them tightly shut. When this latest indignity was accomplished he felt himself being lifted again, up high where yellow fogs swam above a blue sky; strange mists that could not be seen from the ground. But he was in no mood to analyze such mysteries with his eyes clamped shut and head spinning from the speed with which he hurtled through space.

He kept his eyes closed as he slowed down and began to descend. There was a sound of splashing and laughing, with a fresh water smell in the air this time. There was something reassuring about not being dropped on the cold, hard ground. He plopped into a perfectly round little lake.

Fay was never louder than when she was happy. She turned Clive's name into a shout of pure joy and began swimming toward him as he had landed further out than where she and Jennifer had been cavorting. As the sticky gunk washed off his face, Clive opened his eyes to the most welcome sight he could imagine: the real Fay. Or was she?

No one could go through what he had just suffered without the transformation of a perfectly natural wariness into full-blown paranoia. But the delightful vision swimming in his direction sure looked like Fay.

As they made contact, she sure felt like Fay as she put an arm around him and started into her lifesaver act. He felt capable of making it to shore unassisted but did not feel inclined to tell her so. Yes, by the time they came out onto dry land he was sure this was his real sister.

He even allowed himself to notice the obvious. "Fay," he spluttered, "you don't have any clothes on."

"A regular Sherlock Holmes," said Kitnip from her perch atop what had been one of the spider-fish's legs. Clive was glad to see the cat. He was less pleased to notice more evidence that the Land of the Seasons was suffering from severe monster infestation.

Fay stuck to the point by refusing to let her brother get away with being more of a prude than she was herself. "Clive Gurney," she said, hands on hips, "we haven't seen each other since we fell off that stupid mountain and this is all you can say!"

Jennifer emerged from the water next. Clive's eyes were as fishy as the carcass on the beach in that they almost popped out of his head. Jennifer was quite a beauty and in the same state as his sister. "Would you like to swim with us?" she asked.

Before he could put either soggy foot any deeper in his mouth, he was rescued by another large splash in the center of the lake. The dragon had prevented another of Malak's kidnappings but there had been nothing said about whether Clive would be followed.

They watched a small boat rowing toward them with a loan figure hunched over the oars. The dinghy, putting Fay in mind of the one Grandfather had owned, came to rest on the shore. Standing up, the rower revealed himself as another odd character. He was a tall man with a bald head — a football shape rising from the folds of his green cloak, with two little eyes burning in the center. His mouth was a long, jagged scar that was so wide it almost seemed to bisect his face.

"Look, he has safe passage," said Mr. Wynot, cowering in the shallows.

The boatman displayed a white arm band as he came ashore and started walking. There was something wrong about the man's movements, as if he were a machine, a giant wind-up doll. Each time a leg came up, it jerked so violently that it looked to be in danger of coming off. Not until the leg was almost parallel to the ground did it deign to come back down and the other leg perform the same operation.

Clive was all set to run from the marching, robot feet. He'd had enough of the Slaks for one day, although he wasn't sure this was another brand of the same demonic product. But as he could tell from the monstrous remains on the beach, he was hardly alone in facing danger. The others were holding their ground. He would hold his.

The man stopped right in front of Clive and spoke with words like spiders crawling into the ear: "You and your friends are invited to Lord Malak's picnic to celebrate the Seasons." The head turned mechanically, and the sneering mouth added, "Attire will be required."

Chapter Sixteen
The Master's Plan

There was an instant conference with Jennifer, Mr. Wynot, the Tabrik leader and even nervous Mr. Brine. They had dressed for the occasion. Clive and Kitnip kept a watchful eye on Malak's ambassador. Fay was pleased over the way everyone turned to Jennifer for guidance. Whatever these various office holders meant in the grand scheme of things, they deferred to the true representatives of the Seasons. Fay wondered what the other three must be like, and if they encouraged the same degree of confidence as was natural with Jennifer.

"We must go," she said sweetly. "Mrs. Norse has a rule about never being rude, no matter what the provocation." Fay shook her head to clear away the cobwebs and the possibility she'd just heard Jennifer be sarcastic. "Besides, when Lord Malak takes a chance like this he puts himself at risk if he doesn't behave himself," Jennifer finished to a murmuring of agreement.

Mr. Wynot took a moment from vigorously drying what remained of his hair so as to ask a practical question: "How will we get to Summer?"

"We could walk," said Jennifer.

"The picnic will be at Soon o'clock," said the messenger. "Transportation provided upon request."

Jennifer made a command decision: "We appreciate the offer from Lord Malak, but we decline any method of travel that requires his aid. You understand how it is."

The football head remained impassive, but Kitnip felt the fur rise on her neck as if at any moment the robotic man might do something unpleasant. The leader of the Tabriks held up a hand and made an offer: "I'll get us there."

"The invitation does not extend to any of your retinue," said the messenger in an especially snooty manner.

The Tabrik bowed. "Considering how your lord feels about my people, it is wondrous that even I should be welcome."

Malak's man turned on his heel and marched back to the boat. When he had rowed to the center of the lake, he and his craft simply disappeared.

"Let's go," said Mr. Wynot in a merry tone of voice. "At least we'll get a fine meal." He smacked his lips with great gusto.

"You're going to eat his food?" asked Clive warily.

"Yes, my brother's right," added Fay. "Is this wise?"

"The rules, the rules," piped Mr. Wynot. "The enemy is many things but he's never broken the laws of hospitality."

"We'd probably be safe traveling in one of his craft," admitted Jennifer, "but you never know for sure, and I didn't want to give him the satisfaction."

The Tabrik leader gestured for them to follow him and added the reminder, "This way we can take along some of the eggs, in case we need them." He placed strong hands to his forehead and concentrated.

Clive joined Fay as they went off toward the glass hive. They were happy to be together again although she couldn't resist teasing him about his appearance. His shoes were still soggy so he took them off, removed his dripping socks, and put the shoes back on. After wringing the socks out as best he could, he dangled them from his belt as if they were the pelts of dead animals. He was not a happy camper.

Fay wanted to know if he'd seen Wolf. He brought her up to date. They both breathlessly described their adventures — but it soon transpired that Clive had a bit more to relate. Judging herself a newly baptized expert on the subject of water monsters, Fay wanted to compare the spider-fish of the lake to the amorphous entity that Clive had faced at the seaside.Kitnip wanted details about the dragon.

As they neared the city of the Tabriks, Fay pointed at the vehicle that must be meant for their party. Clive thought he was back in Mrs. Norse's kitchen, observing the blue spheres ... except these were much larger and forming a ring around an elaborately rigged glass boat. The seemingly fragile craft came closest in appearance to a gondola, except this was much larger than any of the graceful craft used in the canals of Venice. A ramp was already in place for them. There were advantages to being in the company of the Tabrik leader — advantages as clear as he was.

The spheres pulsed and quivered as they walked up the ramp. Although the seats appeared to be made of hard and unyielding glass (or some sort of transparent plastic) they were, in fact, quite soft. No sooner was everyone seated than the ship rose into the air.

Fay noticed how Clive was gazing straight up with a worried expression. "What's the matter?" she inquired.

"Blue sky overhead," he mused aloud, "but that yellow fog I was drifting in must be up there somewhere. It's the same as what you saw in your dream. And there's that crazy pollen coming out of it with recorded voices."

"You'll drive yourself crazy trying to figure out how anything works around here," she replied. But her words started him pondering the possibilities. Was the yellow fog really above his head, somewhere up high, or was it someplace else entirely? Perhaps it only came into existence when needed. This magic business was more trouble than learning science had ever been. Matters were difficult enough when you had the hope that rules might remain consistent; with magic, the rules might stay the same or they might not.

Clive joined his sister in enjoying the scenery unfolding beneath the prow and was reminded of visiting a national park back home with its fine selection of healthy forests, unpolluted lakes, gently flowing river, neatly kept grounds and other signs of well maintained vitality. And yet there was something subtly wrong with the picture unfolding beneath them: this was one remarkably underpopulated world.

Fay's heart jumped for joy when she caught sight of a lone horse, a white mare galloping in an open field. There were no other horses to be seen.

Clive gently nudged his sister and pointed to a less pleasing spectacle. Several of the diminutive pumpkin men were scrambling for cover underneath a spreading Elm. It was disturbing to think that these little homunculi could enter Spring. He'd hoped they might be restricted to Autumn.

There seemed to be more of Malak's dire creations than the kind of life Fay and Clive wanted to see. Another frustration was that they couldn't get a better sense of geography from this new vantage point than had been the case atop the stone mountain. Beyond a certain point, the picture ended in mist.

Up ahead they had a good view of the peculiar volcano, shrouded in mist, silently belching out the bubbles of light that spread from Summer to illuminate all the Seasons. Clive wanted to climb the thing and see what the view was like. Having spent time beyond the mist, he at least knew there was a *there* there.

Clive wondered if this world might be flat! Certainly it was very much like a big island or small continent, but if he hadn't seen the ocean for himself he would have suspected that the Land of the Seasons was surrounded by … nothing.

A sudden lightness in his stomach and the balls of his feet brought Clive back to "reality," such as it was. Glancing at his sister, he was impressed yet again by her steadfastness.

A dramatic increase in temperature left no doubt as to the location. It was Summer, all right. With a soft thud, they touched down and were greeted by a welcoming committee.

Clive thought he was seeing double, or triple. Three other Jennifers rushed over to embrace their sister who was first to disembark. The Jennifers were not perfectly identical but startlingly similar.

The one in the lead had to be the Jennifer of Summer. She

wore a tight fitting black bikini. The finishing touch was the formality of a black top hat. The other two Jennifers were dressed according to their Seasons as well. The pretty dress and light jacket that went with Autumn seemed a bit out of place in this heat but Clive was most surprised that the one from Winter didn't seem to be burning up in her white parka and hood. Truth to tell, none seemed affected by weather.

After the introductions (a great fuss was made over Fay), the Jennifers led them through a brief stretch of forest. Fay wandered ahead of Clive. He didn't mind in the least. As she pushed some hanging moss out of the way, she was presented with a vision that struck her with such force that it might as well have been a physical blow. He was there, playing host to a large number of people. And he saw her.

Grandfather was dressed in the same black suit in which he'd been buried. Even from this distance there was a musty odor rising from him or from the suit — she wasn't sure which. And yet he'd never looked so young. Perhaps the most incongruous element was that she'd never seen him so relaxed and friendly. Slowly he walked over, with such painful deliberation that it was as if he were moving underwater. She was fixed to the spot, caught in his watery gaze that seemed to crawl up and down every inch of her body.

"My darling girl!" he said as he finally reached her. She pulled back as he tried to embrace her. "Perfectly all right," he cooed. "No need to rush. And look, there's Clive! Hope you have a good appetite, young fella!"

Jennifer of Spring came to the rescue: "Don't overdo it, Lord Malak."

A dark scowl formed on Grandfather's mouth but it was gone as quickly as it had flickered there. For some unaccountable reason, he was exercising self control. "And where is Our Lady of the Seasons?" he asked of this nearest Jennifer.

"Not enjoying your picnic," was the ungracious answer.

"Oh, I understand," he lied, catching sight of Kitnip. "Your Lady would rather stay home with those ... animals."

"Meeeoooow," said Kitnip.

He was wise enough to change the subject: "My, my, you Season girls are all so pretty. How am I to tell you apart if you go swimming? I mean, without your identifying raiment there's no way...."

"Since when would it make any difference to you?" asked Jennifer of Summer in a voice so cold as to belie the heat.

"Well, you girls certainly know how to put an old man in his place. That must include you, mustn't it, Fay?" She bit her lip to keep from making a comment. She was glad at least that Wolf was safe with Mrs. Norse. Malak's sarcasm brought out the best in her.

"Don't pick on her," said Jennifer of Autumn.

Grandfather laughed with the sound of a nest of hornets dying somewhere in the caverns of his sunken chest. "But it's a picnic, dears," he said, his horribly good mood in no way altered. "Very well, I'll behave ... at first. You're all scheming a mile a minute, but let's put all that aside until we've had our hotdogs."

There were several long wooden tables at which disturbingly familiar people were talking and eating. Jennifer recognized the voices before Clive did. She ran over for a closer look. Another family reunion was not what the doctor had ordered, but here it was, in all its grotesque and byzantine splendor. There was a swarm of uncles, aunts, cousins, second cousins, nephews, nieces ... more extended family extending down the length of the tables than she had ever seen all in one place.

She felt a lump in her throat as she recognized the long missing set of her favorite grandparents. And there was her other grandmother, the poor woman who had been ill for so long and had stuck with Grandfather even longer, far longer than sanity would require. Small and trembling, the woman was sitting next to Aunt Miner.

Fay couldn't stand Aunt Miner.

Grandfather came up from behind and took her by the elbow. There was no getting away from him this time. The wild notion that none of this was real — and that they all might be Slaks — was shattered by every scrap of conversation she overheard as he guided her to the head of the table.

A certain kind of inanity can never be faked, such as Aunt Miner declaiming, "But dear, you're not remembering it at all the way it really happened. Donald brought us here in quite a different order. You must have overheard me talking to Cousin Orson and been confused when we...."

Grandfather's grip tightening on her arm, he whispered in her ear, "Isn't it charming, granddaughter, the little things that occupy their minds? Ah, suffer the adults to come unto me."

She pulled away from him and this elicited more Malakian laughter. She never thought there would have come the day when she missed Grandfather's solemn refusal to laugh at anything, but the cruelty of Malak's "humor" had done its work.

"There, there," he said, patting her on the bottom, "just have a seat on the bench there, and I'll attend to the rest." He'd placed a lawn chair at the head of the table and would hold court with Fay at his right hand.

Clive was luckier. He was directed to sit at the next table, every bit as full of distant relatives and Dad's college friends. There were fewer of Mom's friends. She wondered if Mom and Dad might be here, but they were nowhere to be seen.

A sudden flurry of noise drew Fay's attention to a nearby lake, smaller than the one in which she'd been swimming. Maybe this was a monster free zone. She hoped so, for the sake of the children playing in the water.

A volleyball game was starting up at the lake's edge. At first glance the participants seemed to be human, but closer scrutiny revealed them to be Malak's creatures, only better constructed than the ones who had given Clive such a hard time. But the children seemed real enough.

Grandfather returned with her hotdog and a glass of red punch. "I was going to bring you a beer," he said, "but I don't want to get into trouble!"

He draped himself over a lawn chair in a manner so regal that his posture changed what he was sitting on into a throne. The first action he performed was to clap his hands and wait for secret orders to be carried out. The ground rumbled and Fay involuntarily grabbed at the wooden table, receiving a splinter in her thumb for her trouble. Food and drink were spilled every which way.

"You dare not break the laws of hospitality," chimed all four Jennifers as one. They were clustered together at the end of one table.

"This is merely entertainment!" Grandfather assured them, while pointing to the cause of the disturbance down by the lake. A giant statue was rising from the water. The first part of it to appear, like the periscope of a submarine breaking the surface, was the blade of a sword.

I don't believe it, Fay thought angrily, he's doing it again. He must hate swimmers.

Children were running, screaming, from the water. Weirdly, the volleyball game continued, although some of the players had fallen over. That was as clear a way as any of separating the Malak-made from the natural born.

As a giant marble arm came into view, wielding the white sword, Fay remembered where she had seen that limb of stone before: Grandfather's statue guarding his domain in Winter from the Stone Mountain. The appearance of the colossus here was not a good sign.

The cruel head broke the surface as Malak stood, his black suit covered by purple robes he'd yanked out of Heaven knows where, and began to address the assembled company. "Fiends, Humans, Countrythings, lend me your abject support. I am known by many titles: Lord Malak, the Dour One, the Monster, even Grandfather to some, and Uncle, and 'that no good son of a…' well, I am honored by many titles. The time has come to proclaim: Out with the old regime, in with the new and improved. One title will do from now on."

He took a deep drink of the red punch while everyone remained silent and terrified (the next best thing to respect). The statue was up to its waist by now. Grandfather Malak reached under his robes into his jacket pocket and removed a small, brown rock which he then laid upon the picnic table.

"Now this," he intoned, "used to be the Lord High Mayor of Winter."

"I told you he did that!" squeaked Mr. Wynot to the world at large. Jennifer of Winter, eyes watering, cried a thin stream of ice-blue crystals.

"Before this busy fellow went into retirement," Malak continued, "he was critical of my setting up a base of operations in his Season." The speaker glared down the table. "I don't recall anyone objecting when you-know-who built her little house in Autumn. Double standards are always irritating. Anyhow, the mayor of Winter accused me of wanting to be master of more than I ought. Sheer modesty forced me to cut him off before he could elaborate. In his honor, good and gentle beings here assembled, you may henceforth refer to me as Master."

"Even you have never dared break the rules of hospitality," said Jennifer of Spring.

"Shoo, you little pest. No rules have been broken because no one is in danger here, at least not among the invited guests. That's what hospitality is all about. The only conflict is due to…."

"Mrs. Norse," said Fay helpfully.

"Oh, child," his hand snaked out and gently caressed her neck, "you should watch your language. Bad words have a place, but they should be used sparingly."

The statue finished rising from the lake. Some of the young

children, having regained their courage, were gathering again at the water's edge. They were far more interested in the monument to Malak's pride than anything he might actually be saying or doing.

"To continue," he continued, "I should do a little something to consecrate my Masterdom. So it is that I take a moment in this timeless place to let you in on my plan. Both sides of the family are well represented at our little picnic. Without them, I wouldn't be who I was or what I became. My loyal Slaks back on Earth gave me the idea when they reported the unexpected visit of Aunt Miner. So sparing no expense, I invited everyone."

Holding up a hand to staunch non-existent applause, he summed up: "The guests of honor are missing, I grant you, but that will be remedied." He stared at Fay. Then he stared at Clive. "The guests of honor will be with us soon."

After finishing the last of the punch, he threw the cup over his shoulder, confirming more unsavory thoughts Fay held for him. *Litterbug*, she thought. Clive wondered how much dynamite it would take to blow up the statue. He hadn't enjoyed the pleasure of using the exploding pine cones, and would have been very unhappy to realize that Fay had left them behind in Spring.

"I've been the victim of a propaganda campaign, put out by...." Grandfather hesitated, choosing his next words with care, "the enemy. She would have you believe that I'm against the Seasons. Lies, all lies! What I intend to do is take the cliches out of the Seasons and reinvigorate them with a fresh approach. What's so bad about that? I have nothing against Winter, but snow and ice and cold have become a bore! As for Summer, it has its charm ... but why must it always be so hot and humid? Spring has its place, but must it always be warm; and what is more boringly predictable than its freshness, I ask you? Finally, we have the worst cliches of all in Autumn. No wonder the enemy chose to live there. The changing of the leaves is a real yawner!"

Fay concluded that, magical powers notwithstanding, Grandfather was still completely nuts. Enjoying the sound of his own voice, Lord Malak kept right on: "Now I know what some of you are thinking: did he fire six shots, or only five? No wait, sorry about that. Cliches are like a plague. They creep up on you. They're worse than cockroaches. 'Course we're fortunate not to have cockroaches in this pristine world, but do I get any credit for that? I'm the one who emptied the Seasons of its more annoying pests! Bet you didn't know that.

"And I'm working every day to make things better and better. Does the enemy care? Or the dragon, do I get any credit from the dragon? No, and I'll tell you why. Mrs. Norse and the dragon are two peas in a pod; they like things the old way, all messy and ragged around the edges. They claim this world is shrinking when it's obviously the universes that are growing bigger. They blame anything that goes wrong on me. Always it's me! Can you beat that? As for this little world of theirs, it's always been this size. There's a myth that it was bigger once but that's the biggest cliche of them all!"

He had to stop and catch his breath. Row upon row of staring eyes and open mouths brought him back to what passed for his reality. Speaking more softly, he said, "I haven't come to destroy the Seasons. Far from it, I'm offering progress, change, variety. The Seasons have become as boring and predictable as a bad marriage."

He shuddered, then leaned over to Fay and said, "I'm sorry about that, but as you know, sometimes bad language is required for the right effect."

Straightening up again, he clapped his hands. The chest of the giant statue creaked open, revealing two human beings locked in a cage where the idol's heart should be. They were Mom and Dad.

Chapter Seventeen
The Ows In Vows

"Mom," cried Fay. Clive hesitated to speak. "Dad," cried Fay. Clive still remembered how he had been taken in by the Slaks at the village of Il. These two pathetic people, hunched over in a cage, seemed real enough. But he couldn't be sure. Would he ever be sure again?

"They can't hear you," said Grandfather. "I'll bring them to you." There was something terrible about watching Malak enjoy himself. He clapped his hands, as much to applaud himself as to pass on instructions.

The statue began to move. This sent kids scurrying. As before, the volleyball players paid no heed, even after it stepped on one of them as its giant feet SHOOSHED SHOOSHED out of the water, dragging mud from the lake bottom.

Several blood relatives leapt to their feet as if to flee, but with one shouted word of black magic, Grandfather who was Malak held them in their places. He didn't need do much about Aunt Miner. One look at what was causing the commotion and she fainted dead away. Fay couldn't decide if the various friends and family members had any idea where they were.

The gargantuan statue impressed Clive quite a bit, as it continued to press volleyball players into the ground. Back home, he had a picture of the Colossus of Rhodes right over his bed, next to Madonna. There was no sword in that statue's hand but otherwise it was very similar, excepting the face. The THUD THUD of stone feet brought Clive back to the here and now; and he hoped that Grandfather was adept enough with his wizardry to prevent the giant stepping where it wasn't intended. Concern for his parents, if they were his parents, was equally balanced against the personal desire not to be squished. Or squashed.

The statue came to rest a few yards short of the picnic tables.

Fay ran over to it but Clive held back, afraid it might move again. Malak/The Master/The Dour One/Grandfather did nothing to prevent her, and seemed to be encouraging Clive to join Fay. No one else budged from their seats and Clive had the impression of their being held in place by magic. The Jennifers could not be restrained by such means, but they remained seated, heads close together, as if holding themselves in reserve.

Clive finally swallowed hard and took a few tentative steps toward his sister, who called out to him with: "We must wake them up!"

"Their eyes are closed," Clive observed, "but that doesn't mean they're asleep."

"Full marks, Clive," said Grandfather. "You know a trance when you see one. What a promising career you could have had in the bureaucracy of your choosing."

Suddenly dozens of the marching men with football heads appeared. Each carried a piece of long extension ladder. The foremost pushed Fay out of the way.

"Hey," Clive started to protest but Fay surprised him by putting a finger to her lips and shushing him. He went over to his sister and helped her up. The two of them watched the operation. While the football-headed men worked to put the ladder together, hundreds of the smaller jack-'o-lantern men swarmed out of the woods and surrounded Clive and Fay, rubbing them with their soft, spongy hands.

"Just ignore them," said Clive through clenched teeth. He was glad to find out that he was no longer afraid.

"Why isn't Mrs. Norse here to help us?" asked Fay. Clive shrugged as though her absence didn't bother him, but he was worried.

The strange men were bringing Mom's limp body down the ladder first. She seemed to be in a trance. One football man had thrown her over his shoulder, the way a fireman might carry a child he was rescuing from a burning building. Suddenly Fay felt Malak's cold hands on her shoulders. She pulled away.

"Dear children," hissed Grandfather, "only you can save them. I'm giving you the chance to restore your parents' marriage, and help the Seasons achieve their final destiny while you're at it."

"Why should we believe anything you say?" asked Clive angrily.

"When have I told you a lie? Think back to the first day I promised you great things in the future...."

"You never told us what you would do with Mom and Dad," sobbed Fay, turning her face away.

With sophistry worthy of the lawyers he used to decry, Grandfather turned sweet reason into a sour emotion: "Was it my fault you were ripped cruelly from your world, and right after I'd made you masters in your own home? The Slaks were better than your original parents could ever be. They still are! I'd have let you continue bossing them around as long as your little hearts desired."

Fay was about to respond with a kick to the old man's shins when Clive pleasantly surprised her with: "You're a liar, Grandfather! Mrs. Norse said you would have replaced us, too, if she hadn't brought us here first."

"Propaganda, dear boy."

"You wouldn't have left us there long enough to find your stupid gold," Clive went on.

"Well, my dear grandson, at least I approve of your priorities."

Fay wasn't about to let him get away with that. Now it was her turn. "You picked Clive's weakest moment, right after Dad beat him. But Clive already misses Mom ... and Dad, too!"

"How terribly unfair to me," said Malak, "after I rescue the two of you. The marriage was over, children, over except for the formalities. I provided you with the mother and father of your fondest dreams."

Fay ran over to the recumbent form of her mother and cradled the head in her arms, as if she meant to cut off the rasping sounds that came from their mutual tormentor. "Don't listen," she said, as much for her own benefit, hugging Mom harder and harder, as if she could escape that way.

Clive turned from watching his father being brought down the ladder, and faced everyone's mutual problem. "I don't believe you. You hated Dad. You never wanted him to marry Mom. Why would you change now unless it serves your purpose about being Master of the Seasons?"

"Why, next you'll say you don't believe me when I say the sky is blue." Malak sidled over and put an arm around Clive's reluctant shoulders. "What color is it, anyway. Do you think that maybe it's really … yellow, and the blue is a trick?"

Clive shrieked and pushed the bony arms away. His courage seemed to evaporate. How did the vile bastard know about a person's weakest points, the areas you had to force deep down in your mind so they couldn't come back up and haunt your best intentions?

"I've turned over a new leaf," said Grandfather, chuckling at some private joke. "I'm going to make the Seasons better. That's why I was collecting taxes. Improvements don't come free, you know, and it takes a lot of magic concentrated in one special place to get the job done."

Clive and Fay exchanged glances again. The time they'd been separated in this unpredictable world had brought them closer together, if only through comfortable silences they could share. Malak could tell when would-be victims held private councils. There'd been no such trouble with the parents, but these damned (or undamned) kids were a different matter.

"I should never have sent Slaks to offer Clive honest work as a tax collector," he admitted.

Walking over to where Mom and Dad lay sprawled across the grass, he made as if to lift them but actually held them down with a gesture both patronizing and full of anger. He stroked their heads as if they were animals, and pressed down hard so that Mom and Dad's faces were ground into the dirt.

"It's time for us to be a real family again," he said to the prostrate forms. "Already your offspring have grasped the meaning of responsibility to one another. They love. How you poor creatures ever produced two human beings is a mystery, but perhaps we'll find an answer through your sacrifice."

Malak reached inside his ample cloak and, with a flourish worthy of a stage magician, produced two silver daggers similar to the one Clive had seen the Slak version of his mother use on the beach. The Jennifers chose this moment to act. Jennifer of Spring bounded up from her seat so quickly that she knocked over Mr. Wynot, who was so deeply transfixed that he made a little peeping noise as he slid out of his seat. The unhappy man's eyes were glassy, like the rest of the picnic revelers.

Malak was ready for the Jennifers. He drove the daggers into Mom and Dad's backs with the speed of lightning. Fay gasped and tried to move from where she stood but it was as if an invisible hand clutched her, squeezing body and throat hard enough to hurt but not hard enough to kill. Clive couldn't even lift his hand the few inches necessary to touch his sister by the arm in her hour of need.

The Jennifers didn't seem to be trapped the way Clive and Fay were held in place; but the moment the blades were driven home the guardians of the Seasons joined hands and waited for what they knew must come next. Fay's mind was frozen by the spectacle of her parents flailing on the ground, wriggling like bugs pinned to a board. There should have been blood, but the backs of her parents' clothes showed no telltale signs of spreading crimson.

Something else was happening. The hilts of the two knives glowed and formed a single beam of light that touched the sword held in the upraised hand of the giant statue. The stone blade began to glow.

While all this was going on, there was a low sound droning in the background, as if a million bees swarmed a few feet under the ground. Clive could move his arm. Fay turned her head to see him, as the immobility slowly drained from her tortured body. The Jennifers began to chant strange, mellifluous words that provided a counterpoint to the annoying hum, as if trying to keep the sound from growing any louder and driving everyone mad.

Fay was first to notice the new danger. Forming directly over the blade of the stone sword was a small, white cloud. This was the second cloud she had seen in this world. She remembered the last one all too well. She didn't feel any better when she saw a shadow forming underneath the cloud, a shadow in a world without shadows, that resembled a great bloated spider.

The cloud attacked. It fell toward them as if it were made of lead, while thin tendrils reached out from the shadow below, twitching and crawling across the ground. Everyone had noticed Malak's latest monster by the time Fay screamed. Clive grabbed at her and tried to run, but there was no requirement for them to move.

The cloud passed over them, leaving a brief impression of frostbite, before heading toward the picnic tables. As the sky became a source of dread yet again in the Land of the Seasons, Malak chanted: "Takes two to make a marriage; takes two to make divorce; takes two to change the Seasons, and do it with blessed force."

The Jennifers stood between the cloud and the others, staring, chanting their response to Malak in a private language of their own, but the cloud simply zoomed over their heads where it dissipated in the limbs of the trees. A few wisps of white mist drifted away and that was all.

"Good show," said Malak, "pip, pip, and a bit of all right. You, Clive Gurney, yes you there, with the stolid expression, why don't you be the first to investigate my latest masterwork? Don't be shy, just wander over to the nearest tree and check it out!"

Nothing seemed different from his current vantage point, so

he expected the worst. Still, it was a pleasure to be able to walk again. Clive walked over to the trees, brushing past nervous inlaws along the way. The first difference he noticed was a sickly sweet odor that was all wrong. Near at hand was an oak, or something so close it might as well be called one. Reaching out to brush the rough bark with his fingers, he felt the hair stand up on the back on his neck. "It feels real enough" he said as he made contact.

"Everything is real," said Malak who was Grandfather, busily blocking Fay's desire to reach her parents. Whatever invisible force blocked her way was now removed, but he was more than adequate to block her path with his body.

"Be careful," said Fay.

As Clive cautiously plucked a leaf from its branch, he shivered at the touch even though it was still a warm summer day. The leaf rested in his hand as if some marvelous insect that had lost the strength to fly ... in a land that banned insects.

Fay saw his expression change as he gazed down at what was happening in his hand. "What is it?" she called to him, forgetting Malak and her parents as she ran over to him. No barriers blocked her in this direction.

She ran to him as Clive backed away — an incongruous sight, because he was trying to back away from what remained in the palm of his hand, arm held straight out as if it belonged to another person. Coming up behind him, she saw the object of his disgust. The leaf was decomposing. It wasn't turning brown and brittle, as might be expected. Instead, it was liquefying into a muddy orange sludge. The remains made a hissing sound, the part that really bothered Fay. "Throw it away," she told him.

Clive always tried to follow good advice. He let go of it, but that wasn't good enough. Dropping to his knees, he rubbed his hand frantically against the ground.

"You don't have to do that," came the reassuring tones of Malak. "You're not hurt." Clive worked up the nerve to turn his hand over and give it a thorough examination. He seemed to be all right. The same could not be said for the grass that was touched by the liquid as it changed color from natural green to a purple that was neither its color nor the color of the sludge.

Malak was as happy as a clam at a vegetarian convention. He jumped up and down, hooted for joy and talked some more: "What I can do for the Center of All Seasons, I can do for a thousand lesser worlds, feeble reflections of what goes on here; and that includes humble, little Earth, my pretties. Thanks to your parents, dear Clive, dear Fay, I can bring to your world the same originality they worked so hard to bring to their relationship. There's nothing more boring than tranquility, you know!"

Clive wasn't buying a word of it. He grabbed a handful of leaves and ran at Malak, throwing them at his face and trying to mash the rest of them into the wizard's cloak. The Jennifers called out warnings but for reasons best known to themselves, they wouldn't budge from where they continued standing, holding hands. A memory was nagging at the back of Clive's mind like a bad headache, something about a direct approach being unadvisable.

"Aint gonna work on me," said Malak, shrugging off the attack. "I'm immune from my own policies. Like your country's politicians."

"It used to be your country, too, Grandfather!" said Clive as tears started pouring down his face. Fay had never seen her brother cry and the sight made her all the angrier.

"None of that, my boy. We haven't the time. If you want to be patriotic, I'll provide endless opportunity, never fear. But first we must finish the task of Ye Olde parental sacrifice. They're still alive, you know."

Swaggering over to the writhing human bodies, Malak bent down and removed the daggers which made a strange popping sound. Immediately, Mom and Dad lay still.

"Reminds me of their wedding night," he added gratuitously. "The negative energy released by a truly loveless marriage is

not all it's cracked up to be. What we want is a case were love
has gone as sour as yesterday's cottage cheese, but there's still a
little speck of the original passion left. The ambivalence factor
should never be underestimated."

He gestured for one of his football-headed freaks to seize Fay
and bring her over to Mom and Dad. The action was pointless
and cruel as Fay had been struggling to get to them. Clive wanted
to come to her aid but now a football man blocked his passage.

"Fay, you are a mystery to me," he said. "You still love them."

"So does Clive," she felt the need to say. Clive was silent.

"Not the way you do, dear little Fay. Something in the poor lad
makes him judge them. No sense of his proper place, I'm afraid.
Confidentially..." Malak leaned over and did a mock whisper in
her ear, "I never thought you had the potential to be a tax collector the way your brother did. I'd never have sent you to meet the
Maw."

"Thanks so much," she said sarcastically. "Instead I got the
spider-fish thing."

"Nothing but the best for you," he agreed, oozing with charm.
"The kind of love there is in you is a valuable resource. Or as I
read somewhere a long time ago, 'Love suffereth long, and is
kind; love envieth not; love vaunteth not itself, is not puffed up;
doth not behave itself unseemly, seeketh not its own; is not pro-
voked, taking not account of evil; rejoiceth not in
unrighteousness, but rejoiceth with the truth; beareth all things,
believeth all things, hopeth all things, endureth all things.' One
can never be too careful about the books one reads."

Clive chose that moment to chime in with: "Or as ABBA says,
'Breaking up is never easy, I know, but I have to go.'" Clive prided
himself on his knowledge of classical music.

Malak spun around, deeply irate over the interruption. But Fay
was grateful for Malak's distraction because it gave her a chance
to think again.

He was talking about love in its biggest sense, and accusing her of having more than her fair share. He was going to use that somehow to do something dreadful. The lyric from the popular song brought love down to a simpler level. Kids at school were constantly saying they were in love with each other ... and if they were lucky, it would last as long as a hit song on the pop charts.

The caveat was that with everyone worried about AIDS, kids pretended to be less shallow and superficial than they knew themselves to be. For the first time, it struck Fay that Mom and Dad were just about as reliable in the old "love" department as the kids at school. Russell and Claire had simply taken longer to get bored.

This disconcerting view of complete adult bankruptcy took root in Fay with the suddenness of a summer cold. Only she wasn't going to be able to sneeze it away. The idea festering inside her head was that if Mom and Dad had loved their children more, they would have faked marital love to keep the pretense of the family alive.

When adults talked about honesty and rethinking their priorities and getting on with their lives, they arrived at a most interesting place concerning the kids. They expected their offspring to pretend eternal affection; but they wouldn't pretend with each other for the sake of those same children. They'd never extend the freedom of walking away to their kids, either. The police never went after runaway spouses! But runaway kids found out the meaning of being a fugitive in less time than it took to make a fink phone call.

If Malak had known all the trouble that was loosed by Clive's little comment, he would have dumped a bucket of black magic all over his poor grandson. Instead, he turned back to consider Fay, blissfully unaware of the sea change that had just taken place.

"I'll be bringing them back to consciousness just for you," he told Fay. "You can help them do a shallow and temporary reconciliation. When they realize the danger, they'll at least have the sense to go along...."

Yes, Fay thought, fear is the key. That's what had been missing in her parents' lives together: an insufficiency of marrow freezing terror for each other! They needed to spend more time scaring themselves than scaring their kids.

"... but then again, they may be so deeply moved by their predicament, and the sacrifices their children made on their behalf, that the love will be real. If that happens, my master spell won't work. So you have a good motive to do your best. But if they give me what I need, I can release their negative energies, feed that into all the magic I've been hoarding ... and bring the Fifth Season to millions of worlds."

Kitnip sniffed around and said, "Sort of like turning the Universe into a catbox that's never emptied."

"Animal," snorted Malak, no doubt offended by creatures of Kitnip's size who refused to be subordinate. There would be a lot more professionally made Slaks and a lot fewer amateur life forms when he was finished setting Existence to rights.

"There's only one difficulty with your plan, sir," said Fay, smiling sweetly.

"You have no choice, child. The contest is between your hope for their reunion and my confidence in their incompatibility."

"But great Malak, your excellency, sir," Fay said just as sweetly. "What if I've changed my mind? I don't want them back together."

Chapter Eighteen
When You Can't Tell the Problem from the Solution

Fay's words reverberated across the expanse of Malak's face, starting with a twitching around the eyes, trembling to the corners of his mouth that were pulled down into a terrible frown, and quivering through every inch of flesh until reaching the wrinkles around his throat. He was starting to age again. In life, Grandfather had never liked people to stray from roles that he had meticulously written for them. Most folks were true to form ... most of the time. The rare exceptions were the only ones who won his grudging respect, and undying enmity. But since becoming Malak, he had known he could bank on the certainty of Fay's love for her parents.

He was discombobulated, reduced to saying, "You can't mean that."

Clive raised an eyebrow in surprise and was about to contradict his sister when he recognized the impact she had on the enemy. Through thin slit eyes, Kitnip peered at the tormentor's shoes, as black as her fine fur, and let one ear slowly flatten itself against her head. With a sideways glance, Fay caught the reaction of both brother and cat. She had confidence they would play along.

Sensing his uncertainty, she pressed her advantage: "I was tired of Mom and Dad before you died. By the time you ruined my summer, Mom was a coward, and Dad an idiot. I'd put up with them until the day you did weird things to the wall paper in the nursery. Then Dad beat up Clive and Mom didn't do anything to stop it..."

"Maybe she didn't hear," said Malak, trying to salvage the situation.

"She heard! She's a coward and Dad became violent and I don't care what happens to them anymore."

There was the sound of a great sigh out beyond the hills, and several damaged leaves began to curl on their branches as if caught in an invisible fire. The leaves fell off, turning to stinking globs before they hit the ground. Beyond the steaming little piles, the picnickers began to back away, and huddle together.

Terror was like a shot of good whiskey to Malak. His face brightened and regained its composure. "Maybe I've been going about this the wrong way," he said aloud, but he was speaking to himself. "Maybe there's another trigger I can use."

Clive said two words to his sister, but they were all she needed to hear: "Calm down."

She nodded and started taking deep breaths. The ball was in her court. The only way she could score was to be relaxed. Indifference to her parents' fate had bothered Malak; but the anger she was letting herself feel seemed to feed him. Clive held up his hand and she saw that his fingers were crossed. She smiled at him as anger washed over her, and left her body clean.

"I suppose they couldn't help themselves," said Fay. "I'm sorry for them, but they're not my problem any longer."

Malak's sharp intake of breath sounded like a valve being turned off. This would teach him to talk himself! How could a stupid child be so in control of herself? "You don't know what you're saying," he argued, desperation creeping back into his voice. "Those are your parents," he said, gesturing at the ground. "Think how they've suffered."

"They did it to themselves," said Fay, coldly.

"He helped," added Clive, pointing at Malak. "I saw the tortures he inflicted on Dad in the field, and Mom surrounded by little monsters. Those weren't Slaks I saw. They were real, I'm sure of it."

Yet even as he recounted this litany of suffering, he remembered the pictures he had seen of Fay and himself. He was yet to be placed in a box and swung out over empty space. When Fay and he brought each other up to date, she hadn't mentioned being in a giant doll house. His experience by the sea seemed more dreamlike in recollection than his visit to Mrs. Norse's house. In a world where anything could happen, how did one separate symbol from reality? And was it even worth trying?

"Hard lessons," said Malak. "They thought life was going to be easy, an endless summer of love. Perfect examples of their generation, they sought to be eternally young. You know what that means? No experience takes hold and imparts wisdom. They don't remember anything."

"Then what's your excuse for the way you are?" asked Kitnip.

"Be careful, feline. I remember everything."

"Then where's your wisdom?" asked the cat, holding on to the point as she might trap a squirming rodent.

Displaying the same qualities that led his earthbound self into politics, Malak simply ignored the cat's annoying suggestions and again addressed Fay, his focal point, his hope:

"Now look here, granddaughter, you've been through a lot to find your parents. Maybe I was too hard on them. What do you say we bring them out of their trances and you and your brother can have them back just the way you've always wanted them?"

"I don't believe you," said Fay. "You intend to kill them."

"Not so!" he exclaimed.

"What about the knives?" asked Fay.

"There's no blood, no gaping wounds," he answered reasonably. "The most advanced kind of magic doesn't require a lot of mess. Sacrifices don't have to be bloody. They only need to be thorough."

"How do we know they're Mom and Dad?" asked Clive. "Maybe they're Slaks."

"Ridiculous!" Malak seemed genuinely hurt. "Your sister has no doubt in that regard, do you, child?"

But Fay was paying little attention to him. She watched Kitnip who, one moment had been perfectly still as if posing for a statue, and the next was a black streak of motion darting between the legs of Malak's minions.

The cat pressed her nose up against Dad's face. As a cumbersome hand grabbed for her, she leapt over Dad's recumbent form and landed square on Mom's stomach, where she proceeded to investigate familiar human skin and clothes and hair.

"They're real," announced Kitnip.

"And to think you managed that without taking a bite out of them," came a familiar voice.

"Wolf!" shouted Clive, happy and ready for trouble. A silver-grey shape raced out of the woods, four paws barely seeming to touch the ground, and licked the faces of Mom and Dad. Kitnip joined in.

Never one to let an opportunity pass, without at least collecting a toll, Malak made a brave attempt to adjust to the situation. "So there you are," he said. "You see that they're real so let's bring them out of their trances."

"So you can collect their negative energy," said Fay.

"Hey, fair's fair! You get your parents back and I get what I want. A win-win scenario. With all you've learned in such a short time, Fay, I'm sure you and your brother can help them see the error of their ways. Then I'll send everyone home, one big happy...."

"No," said Fay. "You're trying to trick us. Grandfather liked Mom and Dad being unhappy. Malak only cares about his war against the Seasons. You are both people." Malak smiled and made a series of flamboyant gestures in the air, each completed by his pointing at various relatives — his bony finger extended toward the extended family, one member at a time.

"Testimonials," he said. "That's what I need." It was like watching a stage magician who threatened live embalming for the audience as his final act.

"Don't bother," said Clive.

"We don't trust you," said Fay.

"I don't trust them, either," Clive added for the benefit of his relatives.

"The American family is in a bad way," mourned Malak. "Here you trust a total stranger, this self-righteous woman you don't even know, over your own flesh and blood."

"I've met her," said Clive. "Mrs. Norse is only righteous."

"Shut up!" shouted their host.

"All your problems begin in simple rudeness," came another voice, a most welcome one. Malak spun around, dreading to face the inevitable but drawn to his own personal abyss. Mrs. Norse emerged from behind the four Jennifers who, at that precise moment, let go of each other's hands and collapsed on the ground. They had been very busy.

Malak's expression put Fay in mind of a ripe canteloupe ready to collapse in on itself. This was her first encounter with the Lady of the Seasons and she had a most favorable first impression. Where Malak's face was hard and full of judgment, Mrs. Norse's face was a study in long suffering kindness mixed with an unselfconscious superiority.

"You weren't invited," said Malak. The presence of Mrs. Norse drained off his confidence as a syringe might suck up poison.

She spoke to him as firmly and calmly as if she were admonishing a naughty child. "You have forgotten that part of the divorce settlement was that I'd have custody of the Four Seasons." Clive and Fay exchanged looks as if to say: Naturally, Of Course, It Makes Perfect Sense.

"You can stop worrying about the fine points," he said. "Soon there will only be one season."

"You haven't performed your Final Spell, dear, because these young humans haven't behaved as you expected. The first thing we should do is send your audience home."

"I don't care about them," said Malak grudgingly. "They were a sop to an old man's vanity, but they aren't necessary."

Mrs. Norse turned her attention to the brood, still gathered around the picnic tables. She gestured to one, then another, then another. As she caught each one's attention, the individual would step forward, slowly relax, and then vanish. Aunt Miner came last. She took the longest to relax. Apparently the knack of coming and going was tied to an ability for directing conscious attention outward. Aunt Miner needed a distraction from her favorite subject: Aunt Miner. Mrs. Norse provided this by inclining her head toward the great statue. Aunt Miner contemplated the massive bulk and long, straight sword before vanishing home.

"Now to business," said Mrs. Norse.

"You can't stop The One True Season," said Malak.

"I have no intention of putting roadblocks in the way of your Fifth Season," she replied.

"You're not so honest as all that," was Malak's considered response. "To think this poor, sweet child was accusing me of being tricky." He grinned evilly at Fay.

"I don't like being called a child," said Fay.

Malak laughed a most ungrandfatherly laugh, and followed up with: "Tell it to the courts, tell it to your public school ... and God help the first adult who doesn't treat you as a child at all times!"

"Yeah," said Clive. "I guess even bad guys get it right some of the time."

"Evil always has part of the truth," said Mrs. Norse. "But only part. The complete and perfect lie is never adequate in itself to undo Good."

"They must not have many elections around here," Kitnip whispered to Wolf.

"Enough of this!" said Malak. "The divorce agreement puts limitations on you as it does on me. You can't stop the One True Season."

"She can't, but I will!" announced Fay. "You have all this stolen magic but you can't do your magic until Mom and Dad wake up. If you could wake them up, you'd do it. You need me, or

Clive, and we won't wake them up."

Clive thought about Mexican standoffs as he watched two stubborn people — well, one stubborn person and a something else — refuse to give ground. Mrs. Norse kept out of it. The Jennifers, recovered from their exertions, joined the spectators. The football headed men and jack-'o-lantern people held to their positions and waited for something to happen.

"I need you," said Malak at last, "one way or another. You are of Gurney blood. I said that sacrifices need not be in blood. Sometimes the substitute is better. I prepared your parents for this day, and I'd hate for all that work to be wasted. But you are here. And Clive is here. You want to rescue your parents. Wake them and they will at least live. So will you. Leave them as they are, and they will never wake. And as for you..."

He brandished the two silver daggers. "The last time, these left no wounds. They are double-edged, you might say. One side cuts the spirit. But for you, I offer the edge that will release your soul."

Keeping the blade of the left-hand knife flat against his forearm, he held the weapon as if it were a shield. With his right hand, he was already making a great arc with the other blade as he ran straight toward Fay. The moment Malak made his intentions clear, Clive ran toward him, hoping to tackle Fay's assailant, but one of the guards was on him before he had gone more than a few feet.

Fay threw her arms up to fend off the attack, but Malak's speed and size overcame her easily. Wolf and Kitnip ran toward the scene of danger, but too late. To Clive's horror, Mrs. Norse made no move whatever. She regarded the scene with a placidity that seemed criminal to him.

Malak kneeled before the young girl, knocked one of her thin, defending arms away ... and drew the knife with a slashing motion across her delicate, white throat. Clive gasped and stared. There was no red stain spreading like an ink blot under Fay's chin, no dripping crimson finality to mark the passing of her young life. There was a blue glow around the knife and that was all.

"Impossible," said Malak.

"I didn't mean it," moaned a voice much more like Grandfather's.

"The blade that cuts the spirit, my poor, deluded ex-husband," said Mrs. Norse. "You know what that means."

"But how?" Malak's voice was a plea for sympathy but his failure to spill Fay's blood did not win him much in the way of commiseration. "This last sacrifice would create the new Season."

"The Fifth Season already exists," said Mrs. Norse. "It has always existed. You did not create. You discovered a wasteland that you sought to spread across the Land of Life. I could never send you there before now, but you have opened the door."

"The divorce agreement!" He was standing on his rights as only the desperate can.

"Why does it no longer apply?" she asked. He was silent. "As any good attorney knows, never ask a question unless you already know the answer. You could practice magic until you were blue in the face. You could make an army of Slaks and conjure monsters and order foul murders and uncreations to your heart's content. But direct violence by your own hand makes our agreement null and void."

"I don't remember that in the contract," he said. "Maybe you're making this up."

"Well!" she said, offended. "If you doubt me, you can take up the matter with the Dragon. I'm sure he'll be impartial, if he'd ever stopped sneezing. Now, I will pronounce your original name."

He didn't like that. His last words before he faded from view were: "I want the ring back."

"Poor man," said Mrs. Norse, shaking her head. "So forgetful. His previous incarnation stole the ring and turned it into the gold supply this incarnation used to pay expenses."

Raising the subject of money seemed to lift a shroud of gloom from all assembled. Everyone started gathering around and Jennifer of Spring asked if this meant there would be a general refund paid out of the magic surplus. Fay might have found this an interesting subject except that she was too full of gratitude for her life to be concerned about anything else for the moment. And Clive was too thrilled that his sister was safe to care either. Cradling Fay in his arms, Clive rocked her back and forth and whispered how brave she'd been.

"... and so after the current emergency is over, I'd be glad to consider returning the magic," Mrs. Norse finished with a sly grin. Her audience was crestfallen. "Oh, I'm just joking," she said, and everyone heaved a sigh of relief. "Everyone will have their magic back and we'll live happily ever after."

This inspired cheers and hussahs. The Jennifers surrounded Clive and Fay and threw flowers upon their heads. Jennifer of Spring took Fay by the hand and led her to Mrs. Norse. "Thank you for saving us," said Fay.

"Modesty becomes you, young one, but you deserve the credit," spoke a wise heart. "Now, let's have breakfast." Waving to several Tabriks, they came forward carrying trays covered in the exquisite eggs produced by the Klave. These were all brightly colored and looked like Easter eggs.

Suddenly, half a dozen Tabrik ships descended from the sky. Fay regretted that there was no way she could tell which one was the leader as hundreds of them filled the area. She wanted to thank him personally. The grand arrival meant more and more eggs.

In a world without a sun, you tell if you're eating breakfast by the eggs, thought Fay.

Mrs. Norse addressed the company in a voice that seemed loud enough to be heard in all of the Four Seasons: "Thank you, dear Jennifers, for having brought me hither. Thank you, Tabrik friends, for providing the feast. Thank you, Lord Clive and Lady Fay, for your assistance in the defeat of He Who was Malak."

"That was Fay's doing," said Clive.

"You say the right thing, young man, but the honors are for both of you."

"Lord Clive," said Fay, uncertainly.

"Lady Fay," he answered happily. "I guess we'd have a little trouble explaining this in Problems of Democracy at school, wouldn't we?"

They both laughed.

"That's a problem you'll never have to face, unless you want to," said Mrs. Norse. "But first we must resolve the matter of your parents." She walked over and put her hands on Fay's shoulders. A friendly glance in Clive's direction was all he needed to come over and join them. The three of them regarded Mom and Dad, sprawled upon the ground in most undignified postures and sleeping away eternity.

"Fay," said Mrs. Norse. "Tell me something. How should a thirteen year old girl act and talk?"

"Uh…" came out of her in a perfect imitation of one of William F. Buckley, Jr.'s verbal pauses. "I don't know."

"And Clive, how should a fifteen year old boy act and talk?"

"Any way they tell me not to," he said quickly.

Mrs. Norse smiled and patted them both on the head; but instead of feeling patronized and insulted as when Grandfather had performed the same action, they both felt the exact same emotion of joy. Mrs. Norse had that kind of effect on human beings.

"You are both more individualistic than average for your kind," she told them. "This is something to be proud of. You are both of above average intelligence for your species, although Fay is higher than you, Clive."

"You're telling me!" he said.

"Clive's smart," said Fay. "And his grades are getting better."

"Your loyalty is admiral," said Mrs. Norse. "The only test with which I'm concerned, however, is one you both must take here and now."

She kissed Fay on the forehead and then did the same for Clive. There was music welling up from deep inside them. Fay could feel the whole thread of her life running through her, tying the child to the adult, and rejecting the tyranny of what she was supposed to be at given times for given purposes. She squeezed Clive's hand and could tell he was feeling the same power surging through him.

For Clive, the strongest aspect of this emotion was a positive form of defiance, an unwillingness to always say the same words and perform the same actions for no other reason than to satisfy other people. He felt good.

"I don't like the world we've just left," said Clive.

"People say I don't act my age," answered Fay. "I don't understand what they mean. Sometimes they say I'm immature and later they say I'm acting too old. I wish they'd make up their minds!"

"You'll never act your age," said Mrs. Norse, "because you don't *act* at all. You insist on being you. Strange, isn't it, that your parents criticize you for that?"

"I don't like being their son," said Clive. He knew he'd felt that way for some time before his father went crazy and beat him. Yet he'd been unable to eliminate the nagging fear that if he hadn't felt that way, his father wouldn't have sensed it; and through this final disappointment broken the bonds of family.

"You have it backwards, Clive," said Mrs. Norse. "Do you understand better?" she asked Fay.

Fay kneeled in front of the sleeping forms, first brushing the hair away from her mother and then touching her father's cheek. She was their daughter, all right ... but they were also her parents. *Hers.* She let the word sink into her mind as a bathysphere might sink deep, deeper, deepest, into the place where cold secrets wait for one flicker of warmth to rouse themselves and surge upward to be accepted, or to destroy.

"My parents," she said, standing up and facing Mrs. Norse. "They're my parents."

"Yes, child." Mrs. Norse did something with her hands and suddenly she was passing a finished cross-stitch of the Gurney family to Fay. "If you belong to them, then they belong to you," she explained. "As an individual, you have the right to reject anyone and walk off into eternal darkness. But you also have the choice of making your family work as a family."

"That's not true," said Clive angrily, as Fay considered her two problems snoring on the ground. "We have no power over them. That's why I liked it at first when Malak replaced them with Slaks."

"It's not a question of power, but of love," said Mrs. Norse, eyeing Fay as the youngest person there weighed the heaviest burden. "If a family has love, then whatever member is best qualified to make a correct decision is heeded. The reward is survival, as a family. If it is the father some of the time, or most of the time, or all of the time, then it is the father. If it is the mother some of the time, or most of the time, or all of the time, then it is the mother. If...."

"Yeah, I get the idea, but it doesn't work," said Clive. "If it's the daughter or the son, they're never listened to."

Mrs. Norse was most insistent: "If love is present, then they are heeded. The family without love deserves to be destroyed. Some blame this reality on God. Some blame it on Nature. But whatever word is used, this is the reality."

"Ours should be destroyed then!" said Clive. "We have a terrible family. I hate us."

"No!" Fay spoke in voice as strong as Mrs. Norse. His sister reached out and touched him by the arm, telling him in no uncertain terms, "They're just weak, Clive. I don't want them dead. Or us. I want them strong."

"Yay," said Kitnip, "put them out of the house if they make a mess."

"Rub their noses in it first, and then throw them out," agreed Wolf.

Fay took Clive by the hand. She didn't say a word but looked him in the eye. It was as if their shared pain ran back and forth along their arms, and gradually Clive allowed a smile to write itself across his troubled face.

"Let's wake them up," said Fay. "How do we do it?"

Mrs. Norse gave Clive and Fay one egg each. She motioned for them to feed the parent of their respective sex, as though Fay were responsible for Mom and Clive for Dad. The eggs broke open easily and a rich foam poured out. Fay fed her mother, slowly, and the middle aged woman opened tired eyes that held in them a glint of hope. Clive just dumped Dad's food down him in one go, and the man started up as if waking from a dream. He blinked at the cool blue sky, and then saw the anxious faces of his offspring.

"Who are you?" asked Dad.

"Who are you?" asked Mom.

Then they looked at each other with equal confusion.

"This is not true amnesia," said Mrs. Norse. "In time, they will remember everything. But this way you will guide them as they recover ... themselves."

"Are we going home?" asked Clive.

Mrs. Norse nodded her head slightly, first to Clive and then to Fay. "That's up to you. But you may stay here in the Land of Seasons if you prefer, as Lord and Lady of the realm."

There was an intense discussion of the pros and cons of the choice thus presented. Sixty seconds later, if anyone had had a watch to arrive at such a figure, Lord Clive and Lady Fay reached a decision. They would stay. The Jennifers celebrated by dancing, weaving their hands through the air as if making invisible sculptures.

Mom and Dad sat down with the rest and ate some more eggs. Fay liked the taste of them better than Clive, but Mrs. Norse suggested that she might be able to rustle up something like salt to improve the flavor. Later, Fay began the first lesson, carefully telling Mom and Dad their Christian names and how they'd been married.

"What's marriage?" asked Mom.

"It's a promise made in love," answered Fay, feeling older and smarter with every mouthful of the Tabrik's food.

"What's love?" asked Dad.

"Another promise," said Clive, feeling stronger and happier for dessert.

"And these are promises where you don't cross your fingers," added Mrs. Norse.

Then Mom and Dad were told what happened to people who broke their promises. In a land of magic, the possibilities were varied and quite interesting. Mom and Dad promised to behave themselves.

Epilogue

Aunt Miner found the gold. She wound up buying both the house and Grandfather's summer cabin on the lake. Then she went into business with Bob Cohen's computerized astrology and marriage counseling. She is doing quite well and has had offers to appear on Geraldo and Oprah. The only subject she won't discuss is how she came into possession of two very convincing clay statues of Russell and Claire Gurney.

THE END

About the Author

Brad Linaweaver is author of the Prometheus award winning novel, *Moon of Ice*, which was also a Nebula finalist when it appeared as a novella in *Amazing Stories*. Published in America and England, the novel opened the door to his full time career as a writer.

He's sold over sixty short stories to magazines and anthologies, the latter including *Adventures in the Twilight Zone, Peter Straub's Ghosts, Superheroes, Miskatonic University, Confederacy of the Dead, Dark Destiny III: Children of Dracula, Alternate Warriors, Alternate Generals, Alternate Americas, Hitler Victorious, Tales from the Great Turtle, Psycho-Paths* and *Pawn of Chaos*. His first short story sale to an anthology was "Shadow Quest" in *Magic in Ithkar 2*, edited by Andre Norton and the late Robert Adams.

He is author of *Sliders, The Novel* and *Sliders, The Classic Episodes*, from the popular television series. With Dafydd ab Hugh, he is co-author of four popular *Doom* novels, based on the video game from id Software. He is currently working on his first *Wishbone* book.

In addition to media tie-ins, he works more directly with film and radio! He had a radio play on National Public Radio as part of the *Horror House* series. He shares story credit with producer Fred Olen Ray on *Jack-O*, the last film of John Carradine. (He also co-edited the anthology *Weird Menace* with Fred.) He adapted Robert A. Heinlein's "The Man Who Traveled in Elephants" for the Atlanta Radio Theatre in a production starring Harlan Ellison and introduced by Ray Bradbury. He has performed with Turhan Bey, David Hedison, Michelle Bauer, Brinke Stevens, John LaZar, J. J. North, Forrest J Ackerman, Robert Carradine, Don "the Dragon" Wilson, Brittany Rollins and Leslie Culton. He's been on HBO and the BBC.

He's done over two hundred non-fiction pieces, appearing in *National Review*, *Chronicles*, *The Atlanta Journal & Constitution*, *Locus*, *Cult Movies*, *Femme Fatales*, *Filmfax*, *Famous Monsters of Filmland*, *New Libertarian*, *The Agorist Quarterly*, *Spacemen*, *Synnwatch*, *Florida Magazine*, *Reason* and many others.

He is co-editor with Ed Kramer of *Free Space*, the only libertarian science fiction anthology in the universe.

www.ingramcontent.com/pod-product-compliance
Lightning Source LLC
Chambersburg PA
CBHW030522020726
47494CB00004B/1192